DATE DUE			

Aspects of Love

Aspects of Love

David Garnett

Alfred A. Knopf   *New York*   1990

To

ANGELICA VANESSA GARNETT

Part One

"**Alors,** *je te laisse cet enfant charmant. Sois gentille avec . . . on dirait que c'est son premier amour,*" said the fat French actor as, after giving Alexis his left hand, he tapped Rose affectionately twice on the cheek and left them together at the café table to step into the street where rain was still falling and the puddles reflected the street lamps on the boulevard. Then, when he was already some yards away, he turned to call back to her in a loud voice: "*On se reverra à Albi dans la quinzaine.*"

Rose made no effort to reply, or to show that she had heard his words, but watched him disappear with a sombre expression. She seemed unaware of the boy sitting opposite her and she would indeed have got up and left him without a word if she had not been afraid of wetting her only decent pair of shoes and splashing her nylon stockings.

The population of Montpellier had proved disastrously indifferent to Ibsen, so that Marcel had had to bring the projected three weeks' run of *The Master Builder*, *The Doll's House* and *Hedda Gabler* to an end after only six performances and they were not due to open their week at Albi for another fortnight. The little company of earnest young actors and actresses was stranded. Rose had borrowed two thousand francs from the leading actor, Paul; Marcel had advanced her another two, but to live for a fortnight on four thousand francs and get herself to Albi was impossible. The rest of the company were going back to Paris and as she had had a violent quarrel with all of them, she had concealed the fact that she had no money. She would have to pawn her clothes, and when the rain stopped, she must find herself a new lodging. Better stay at Montpellier than hang around for a fortnight with nothing to do in Albi.

Absorbed in these gloomy thoughts, she had forgotten her companion and looked up with surprise when he said quietly:

"Where are you going to live until you go to Albi?"

She made no reply except to shrug her shoulders slightly. His French was correct and his English accent more agreeable to her ears than that of the Midi. He was handsome also: pale grey eyes contrasting with his dark hair, black eyelashes and swarthy skin. Rose remembered seeing him sitting in the front row of the empty stalls every night holding a bunch of flowers which he threw on to the stage before the curtain. How typical of Marcel's evasive tactics to have brought an infatuated schoolboy along when she wanted to have a straight talk: to tell him that her loyalty to highbrow drama would not stand being stranded penniless for a fortnight. Why should she go to Albi? How dare he presume that she would turn up? Let him stew in his own juice! Albi! A wretched little town. What hope was there of playing Ibsen to a crowded theatre there even for a week?

The waiter was hovering about them. "Would you like a liqueur?" asked the English boy uncertainly.

"Coffee—*croissants* and butter—and an *Armagnac*," she said in a firm, almost unfriendly tone. It was all the supper she could hope for. Alexis gave the order and added: "A glass of white wine for me."

So her young admirer was not rich. Rose looked at him again and for the first time since Marcel had come to fetch her from her dressing-room and had introduced the stage-struck boy, she smiled at him.

"If I am not very nice to you it is because I have things to worry me. But thanks for the flowers every night."

"Have you any plans for the coming fortnight?" he asked in a voice which was timid but persistent.

The boy was going to be impertinent! She looked

at him fiercely, but all at once her feelings changed. He was a child, and perhaps what Marcel had said in front of him was true.

"No. None. And very little money."

"Will you allow me to make a suggestion?"

She lifted her large green eyes and stared into his grey ones. He could not be much more than seventeen. Then, as she did not reply, he explained breathlessly.

"You see, I have an old uncle who has a villa at Pau. It has been shut up since before the war. We could live there together until you have to go to Albi. I would suggest a hotel at Cannes or Nice, but I have no money either."

"What a wonderful idea!" cried Rose, suddenly delighted. "Marvellous. But what will your uncle say when he finds out?"

"You will have gone to Albi long before that. It won't matter. I know the old gardener."

Her mood had changed completely. Why not accept? The boy was charming. It was his first love affair, obviously. Well, she could be very nice to him ... Not another night in this hateful city which had ignored her performances of Hedda and of Norah.

"Are you sure you want me to accept?" she asked. This time it was the boy who was silent. Rose saw him swallow with an effort and noticed that he had turned pale.

"All right, then I accept. Here, drink a drop of my brandy."

Five minutes later they parted, she to pack her trunk and leave her lodgings; he to collect a few of his possessions secretly from the pension where he lodged.

As soon as they had separated, a horrible fear possessed each of them that the other would not turn up at the railway station.

"Well, I shall leave Montpellier anyway," Rose said to herself. "It will be cheaper living in some little town." But it was with a deep breath of relief that she saw Alexis come through the entrance and look about him uncertainly.

"I thought you would have changed your mind," he said.

"I thought you would not come," she replied, and taking him in her arms, she gave him a kiss which left him trembling.

"We get there at five o'clock in the morning," he said. "It will make it easier for us to break in unobserved."

Rose burst out laughing. "Have you seen Charlie Chaplin's *Modern Times?*"

"I promise you my uncle's villa is nothing like the shack they set up house in," replied Alexis seriously.

Rose laughed and her whole character seemed to change as she said:

"What a goose you are. I didn't mean that. I meant

that we should spend our fortnight in and out of gaol. By the way, what is your name?" It was the first time she had called him *tu* and once again she saw him go pale.

"Alexander Golightly, but I've always been called Alexis," he said.

Then he smiled as though with an effort and said:

"No. It is quite true about my uncle. He won't send me to prison. He is a Baronet—Sir George Dillingham. He's fairly rich, and a poet. But he has never been back to the villa because his wife died during the war. She was an actress and a very famous beauty, much older than him, may have been King Edward's mistress."

In the train they were already sweethearts. She slept for an hour or two with her head on his shoulder, her body slack with the physical intimacy of fatigue.

Alexis was too excited to feel tired: he gazed at the fittings of the third-class compartment and it seemed to him that he had never been in a train before. The rhythm of the wheels on the lines, and the strokes of the engine, its sudden checks, creaking of brakes, the slow bumping to a halt, the great wheels spinning before they gripped the lines and the strain of starting; the sound of a little trumpet not far off in the night, the slow acceleration, all the familiar sounds took on a new meaning and were the perfect accompaniments to an unbelievable romance which invested them with its own significance and beauty. Later he reflected: "I shall never be able to hear the sounds of a French train again, without living through these moments!"

The first light of dawn showed through the dirty windows. Fields, lines of poplars, the vague indications of a passing signal box or a farm, steeped in colours more subtle and exciting than those of day, made their appearance. The watching boy suddenly slipped his hand into his coat pocket and, feeling the heavy shaft of a metal packing-case opener, smiled for the first time that night. The touch reassured him: it would be all right. Soon afterwards he fell asleep.

Rose lifted her head and looked about her and as she did so, Alexis's head sank heavily upon her shoulder and their positions were reversed. For the first time she was able to study every feature of his face unobserved. The gentle rise and fall of his breathing, the weight and warmth of his body leaning helplessly against hers was a delight, and her lips curled as she wondered: "Supposing, after all, it was I who fell in love with this poor child playing truant from school?"

At last, almost angrily, she pushed him upright and lifted his head so that it balanced insecurely, while she felt for a scent bottle, dabbled her face with eau-de-cologne and powdered it. The train began to reduce speed: Rose looked at her watch, tapped Alexis on the shoulder and he woke at once, completely in possession of his faculties.

"Pau."

Les Pervenches was on the outskirts of Pau and a long way from the railway station, most of it uphill. When she was halfway, Rose took off her shoes and stockings and carried them. She waited speechless with exhaustion while Alexis, working with the packing-case opener that he had brought, broke the locks fastening a french window. She was past caring what happened to her as she followed him uncertainly upstairs. The corridor was dark and she almost dozed off while he broke open a bedroom door. Then he pulled her to her feet and they both lay down on a bed covered with a dust-sheet and fell asleep without exchanging a word.

Alexis woke suddenly, fully aware of all around him. A thin shaft of sunlight falling through a crack in the shutters revealed the disorder of the darkened room filled with pieces of furniture which had been pulled forward from the walls, each under a dust-sheet. Beside him Rose was lying upon her back with her legs apart and one arm doubled up behind her head. Her full breasts rose and fell under her blouse as she breathed. As he looked at the unconscious almost expressionless face, streaked with dirt, the boy clenched his teeth with fierce determination. Then, with delicate movements he slipped off the bed and tip-toed out of the room. There was an immense amount to be done: a room must be made habitable and breakfast provided before she woke.

Four hours later he was still at work when Rose

woke up and looked about in astonishment at finding herself fully dressed amid the dirt and lumber of an unknown room.

"I must have been mad last night and I'm further away from Albi than ever. Well, I'll find my bag and clear out." She rose to her feet, winced with pain, and set out to explore the villa. If, at that moment, she had come face to face with Alexis, she would have hissed at him with anger. But when she stepped into the carpetless passage something even more ravishing than the warm mid-day sunshine struck upon her senses: the smell of coffee. As she walked downstairs her mouth watered and when she opened the door of the kitchen she saw that the table was laid: a jug of coffee and one of hot milk were on the table; there were bowls and butter and Alexis was toasting rolls before a glowing grate.

"I was just going to call you. I've been out and I've a lot to tell you."

She did not ask him his news, or speak of her determination to leave the villa, because the taste of the bowl of hot coffee was so good that she simply had to roll her eyes and smack her lips. Later, when he had filled her bowl again, almost involuntarily the words popped out: "Darling, come and let me give you a kiss. You make the most marvellous coffee."

Was that what she felt, after all?

A little later Alexis said: "It's not only the coffee . . ."

Rose went into a ripple of laughter. "So he is becoming vain. He thinks he is wonderful in all sorts of other ways."

He looked at her sharply with an odd smile and replied: "If one cup of coffee can buy a kiss like that, what will you give for *pâté de campagne*, half a cold chicken, a fresh salad and a bottle of *Gaillac*?"

"That sounds good. If I'm still hungry I shall eat you up for dessert. Be careful, my boy, I am a man-eater," said Rose, laughing. Again she saw the colour fade out of the boy's face and at the sight of his emotion a feeling of compunction overcame her. He was buying her love, for if there had been no breakfast she would have gone away. She must be tender and gentle and not make a joke of it.

"You have done all the work while I have been asleep. Now I'll do my share. If you will help me move the furniture I will clean out the bedroom before we have our lunch. You have made me feel strong again."

As they dragged the furniture into the corners of the room, swept and dusted and finally made up the big double bed, he told her his news.

When he had gone out into the garden he had at once met *le Père* Jerôme, the old gardener. "He recognised me, of course, and asked me where I had come from. So I replied: 'Haven't you had my uncle's letter? I was expecting you to have lighted a fire.' Jerôme mumbled a bit, so I said: 'Well, he has lent me the villa for a holiday. I have some friends coming later on. Now you go into town and buy me some things.

I'll give you a list. And tell the electricity people to come and connect up the current at once.' So I wrote out a list of necessaries and sent Jerôme off with it. So now we are well established."

"How did you pay for all the things?"

"Pay? Why should I pay? Old Jerôme's credit in the town is excellent. The bills will go to my uncle and in the end he'll pay, I suppose. But we must be reasonable in our demands. No mink coats and diamond necklaces."

"I was just going to give you a kiss for being so clever. But I won't now," said Rose.

He saw that his words had upset her and they worked in silence. At last he said: "I did not mean that you were mercenary ... and you can have a mink coat if anyone is fool enough to trust *le Père* Jerôme with one."

She laughed and, giving Alexis a quick kiss, said: "What about the pâté and the chicken?"

It was late afternoon by the time they had finished the lunch washed down with the delicious cool regional wine and Rose had asked for and been given a cup of coffee. When she had finished it she said: "Have you forgotten my dessert?" It was a moment before Alexis understood her words. Then he flushed and turned pale again. They went upstairs silently and Rose proved very gentle and tender with him. At last they lay too happy to speak, too full of speculations to go to sleep and too closely entwined to look at each other.

"What were you doing in Montpellier?" asked Rose eventually.

Alexis pondered for a little and answered: "I got expelled from my public school last year—the usual reason. So my uncle brought me over to France. I don't think he wanted me hanging about in Paris, so he invented a theory that the real France is only to be found in the Provinces and sent me to the University of Montpellier instead of to the Sorbonne. Of course I've lived in France as a child quite a lot, before the war. I could talk French really well when I was eight years old. I'm to go in for the Consular Service."

Rose asked what he meant by "the usual reason" and laughed a good deal when Alexis explained.

Some time after the sun had set, Alexis got up, put on his coat and trousers and went downstairs to make up the stove and lock up the house. He brought back a bottle of white wine which they sipped alternately from the same glass.

Before Alexis fell asleep that night he had discovered what Rose had meant when she called herself a man-eater. "She has changed the whole world and hung a curtain between the present and the past," he thought. Five minutes later she whispered, "How could I guess that a boy like you could make me so happy? You know I nearly ran away from you this morning." But Alexis was already asleep.

They were awakened by the man from the Electricity Supply hammering on the door. Later *le Père* Jerôme brought them a basket of vegetables, was introduced to Rose, and offered to go into the town again for them. He said nothing about not having received Sir George's letter. He made Rose a present of a basket of wood strawberries and took the opportunity of having a good look at her. While she thanked him prettily his coarse old face was wreathed in smiles, but as he walked back to his hoeing he spat and remarked:

"I'd rather have a stuffed leg of lamb myself."

That morning they began to explore the villa and its surroundings. Though *Les Pervenches* had been built about 1900, it had some of the elegance of the architecture of fifty years before. Two pairs of french windows opened out of the dining-room into a little verandah, above which was a balcony, both made of ironwork which was now covered with clematis and passion-flower and shaded on one side by a huge magnolia in full bloom. The garden had originally been laid out in formal prettiness but since the war had been given over to rows of lettuces, fennel, sorrel, dwarf beans and globe artichokes. Under a cypress they discovered a stone pedestal supporting the lead figure of a Persian cat with the inscription: *Ci-gît Cyrus, Roi des Persans, 23 Mai 1916*. Rose and Alexis looked at the monument for a few moments in silence and went indoors. The lead cat and particularly the date—long before either of them had been born—

depressed them. What record would there be of either of them in another thirty-two years?

The room with the balcony proved to be large, with dust-sheets hung round three sides of it. Behind these were bookcases full of books. While Alexis was beginning to look at them Rose opened the french windows on to the balcony and stepped out. In front of her was a magnificent view of the distant Pyrenees with a jagged outline of sharp peaks and in the foreground, broken hills covered with forest. Rose stood staring silently. The pettiness and pretentiousness of human existence lay below her feet and in the rooms of the villa, but the view of those jagged peaks and tumbling forests changed its whole character. They were a reminder, and an acknowledgment on the part of the inhabitants when they looked out, of the wild eternal forces of the spirit that she felt in herself.

Alexis spoke and she called to him: "Come out here."

He stepped out and she said: "That is what I feel I ought to be when I am acting."

Her words seemed to Alexis exaggerated: he had seen the view often before when he had been a little boy. It reminded him of his uncle. But he could see that Rose was feeling a sincere emotion. If she had said that the mountains were like their passion for each other he would have understood it and shared it. But it was her ambitions that they symbolised and that she was thinking about.

"My uncle George never lives anywhere unless there is a magnificent view," he said.

"I think I should like your uncle," Rose replied.

"Come and look at his library. I had no idea it was so complete. I suppose he must mean to come back and live here one day," said Alexis. After they had looked at the books they went upstairs and in the attics found all Lady Dillingham's dresses stored away in three metal uniform cases between layers of tissue paper plentifully sprinkled with moth balls.

Rose was fascinated and could not tear herself away from them. So Alexis left her in order to cook dinner. When the globe artichokes and the waxpod beans were ready and the eggs beaten up and ready to go into the pan with the mushrooms and the herbs, he called up to her. But it was some moments before Rose appeared, wearing one of the evening dresses she had found which made her look like a mermaid being presented at the court of Edward and Alexandra. It was of blue satin with green sequins, cut very low in the *corsage*, full in the hips and tight round the knees and then spreading into a fishtail train. Alexis stared at her speechlessly and Rose said: "Darling, you must come and hook me up behind."

First, however, he made her a ceremonious bow and kissed her hand. *"Enchanté, Madame."*

When he had finished with the hooks, Rose threw herself back into his arms.

"Kisses or omelette?" asked Alexis.

The words came out between his clenched teeth. It was, he felt, decisive. "Kisses or omelette?" meant at that moment equality: that he was a man, not a child at Rose's beck and call, to be kissed at one moment and thrust aside at another.

Rose, however, did not completely understand what had lain behind the words.

"Omelette every time of course," she answered, laughing. But Alexis did not laugh. With his mouth still set and his teeth clenched he went into the kitchen, put the frying-pan on the hot-plate and brought the globe artichokes and the *vinaigrette* sauce into the dining-room.

Rose looked at him with a speculative eye. "He has a strong character. I don't like weak men," she reflected, when he had gone to make the omelette.

Later when they were eating the wood strawberries which old Jerôme had brought that morning, Alexis said: "We have a wardrobe of dresses and a library; why don't we act a play?"

Rose clapped her hands: "You are a genius. Marcel wants to put on *L'Occasion* by Mérimée. We can practise and I shall be given the part of Doña Maria the young Spanish girl. You must act Fray Eugenio the priest."

Alexis ran upstairs and after a while returned with the book. For an hour or two they skimmed through the play, skipping and reading only the scenes in which there were no other actors.

"We'll spend tomorrow rehearsing," they repeated

as they went to bed. For a long time they lay in each other's arms: love was too sweet, the night too precious to be given up to sleep ... and yet neither of them had the strength or the desire to stir.

Suddenly there was the sound of a footstep on the attic stairs, one followed by another. Then came a third.

They lay still. Their hearts were racing. They were filled with wonder, spiced with terror.

Clump ... clump ... clump.

Hesitating, irregular, sometimes loud and sometimes softer, the footstep descended, one stair at a time.

"It's her ghost. I'm frightened," whispered Rose.

"Nonsense," replied Alexis, although gooseflesh was spreading from the nape of his neck on to his shoulders. But the steps had stopped. For five minutes the lovers lay silent, scarcely daring to breathe. Then came two more steps just above the landing outside their door.

Suddenly Alexis threw himself out of bed, switched on the lights and flung open the door. There was nothing. Then, when he had switched on the light on the landing, he saw that on the bottom stair there was lying a lady's green morocco high-heeled shoe, one of a pair that Rose had unpacked and left on the attic floor. Alexis stared at it open-mouthed. Its presence produced a disagreeable sensation, but he immediately realised that it would confirm Rose's fear that the villa was haunted and that if he told her about it she might refuse to stay there any longer with him.

He left the shoe lying where it was, switched out the light on the landing, and went back into the bedroom.

"Well?" asked Rose.

"There's nothing there. I suppose it may have been a rat," he said.

"I can't sleep in a house full of rats," said Rose.

"I don't want you to sleep just yet," said Alexis.

"Oh, but I mean it. I don't like rats."

"Think about something else."

"I suppose I must," she answered, looking at him.

Already Alexis had got over his moment of terror, though he still believed that what they had heard was his aunt's ghost. Next morning he took the shoe up to the attic where its fellow was lying and put them both back in the big black metal box and shut it. They were not disturbed again.

For the following days they read and rehearsed *L'Occasion*. But every day, after they had finished lunch, Rose said:

"I want my dessert," and they would go upstairs together in the empty house. Neither of them spoke and there was in this silence something ritual and apart from life:—the darkened room a temple, Rose its priestess, he, blindly obedient, the chosen victim for sacrifice and rebirth. The sunlight fell in narrow bars through the closed Venetian blinds, there was a smell of moth balls and old leather. Rose always began by kissing him until he could bear no more. His heart and senses were too full for happiness or pleasure. White limbs laid upon the altar, a knife plunged into a beating heart, a God breathing new life into the nostrils of the sacrifice: such were the only symbols for such ecstasy.

And afterwards, when Rose was sipping the cup of tea which he always made for her, she would yawn, showing a little tongue which curled at the tip like a kitten's, and then say reflectively:

"You are exactly what I want. With you it is perfect."

And Alexis, pretending not to hear her words, would pick up the volume of Mérimée and say: "Here is your cue."

It was an unconscious relief to be working with her and not thinking about making love at every moment.

"We can have a dress rehearsal this evening," said Rose, nine days after their arrival, as she sipped her tea. "I shall finish hemming your *soutane* before dinner."

The old Rolls stopped noiselessly outside *Les Pervenches* and Sir George Dillingham got out. He was a lean figure in a loosely fitting Shetland tweed suit of blended grey and moorit wool; he wore a tussore silk shirt with a Leander tie pulled through a heavy gold and aquamarine ring. When he had received *le Père*

Jerôme's letter two days before, he had felt quite un-
reasonably angry. The real reason for this was a
purely personal one. He had just met a young Italian
widow, the Marchesa Trapani, at the house of an artist friend in Paris. He had been immensely charmed,
and she, he thought, was attracted by him. If he left
Paris she would have probably gone back to Venice
before his return and it might be difficult to meet her
again. But as he had not admitted to himself that his
feelings for Giulietta were serious, his exasperation
found other outlets. He was angry not only with his
scapegrace nephew, who had got himself expelled
from school, but with his sister who had died five
years before, leaving him as the boy's guardian, and
with his own mother who had died two years before
Alexis was born, for thrusting Milly into smart society
and then encouraging her to marry a wastrel who had
died leaving her nothing.

Such feelings were a waste of time, but they suf-
ficed to start him on his journey. In the two days he
had spent driving down from Paris, his anger with
Alexis had changed, first to boredom and then to cu-
riosity. But he wished he had not come and was uncertain what he proposed to do. He wished he had
not come, not only because of his nephew but because he would have to face the question of when, if
ever, he was going back to live at Pau. He had waited
for three years since the war, unable to bring himself
to sell the villa, pretending that he intended to settle
there some day. But it was painful to see the place

again; it would be unendurable to be continuously reminded of the past. Probably he ought to decide to sell it. But first he must deal with his nephew's escapade.

"I had better see how the land lies before I start playing the heavy father," he said to himself. "Of course it is a hundred to one that the girl is just a tart he had picked up in Montpellier—though I don't know where he can have got the money for her. But girls have changed a bit since I was a lad—she may be a little bourgeoise typist, or even a lady. Anything is possible. They may not even be going to bed together. I must have what they call a 'looksee'."

But in practice 'having a looksee' meant spying on a pair of lovers—an occupation that Sir George had never conceived it possible for him to be engaged in, and against which his instinct revolted. Thus after walking stealthily into the garden he came to a halt, took a few steps on tiptoe and stopped again, disgusted.

The night was warm, the french windows of the villa were open and a broad band of light poured out upon the spiky rows of artichokes where once there had been a tennis lawn.

The sight of these vegetables left him aghast. He knew that old Jerôme had turned the garden into a market garden during the war and had brought up his family upon the proceeds. But digging up the tennis lawn was going rather further than he had expected.

He could not possibly complain and he knew it was

unreasonable to feel annoyed. But he was upset: the sight of the artichokes took the last grains of his resolution away. He felt saddened and disgusted and very loath to face his nephew.

"Oh, bloody hell take the little brute. I've a good mind to go back to Paris without seeing him or saying anything—and let him have his fun—and run up bills at my expense. But it's a bad habit to get him in the way of," Sir George muttered to himself.

"I suppose I had better just walk up to the front door and ring the bell." But at that moment a clear and surprisingly distinct man's voice sounded from the drawing-room.

"What does this letter contain? Give it me." Sir George did not recognise it as that of his nephew because he was speaking fluent French with little trace of an English accent.

"But promise not to read it while you are here. Read it this evening—wait till the evening." It was a beautiful female voice and the tone was proud, humble, childish and despairing.

"Promise me. And tomorrow ... no, never speak to me about it. If you give it back, don't say hard things to me ... It would be no use. Just give it back to me ... and I shall punish myself for my folly ... But for God's sake don't scold me ..."

"Hand it over." The man's voice was hard.

"Have pity, I implore you. I've resisted as long as I could. But you mustn't open it here. Oh, God, what are you doing? Father Eugenio, I implore you. For pity's sake, give it back. Father, you are killing me. Don't read it here."

"What are you doing? Pull yourself together," said the man, and then added in a horrified whisper: "There's somebody coming!"

Further concealment was impossible, and Sir George stepped into the lighted french window and looked into the room.

A young priest in a black *soutane* and wearing a skull-cap was facing an extraordinarily pretty girl wearing a short petticoat and a Spanish shawl with a lace mantilla on her head. What struck him most was the contrast of her colouring: large brilliant green eyes and dark rusty red hair. For a moment they did not notice his appearance and in those few seconds Sir George had time not only to realise that he had been listening to a play but to remember it as Méri-mée. It was a moment longer before he recognised his nephew. While he was still staring, motionless, both the young people looked up and saw him standing there.

"Please excuse me for interrupting," he said, speaking in French. "It's astonishing that you should be acting . . . and am I right in thinking that it is a scene from that little play of Mérimée's? You are admirable, Madame. From the few words I overheard . . ." His remarks died away and silence followed.

"I suppose old Jerôme wrote to you about my being here," said Alexis in English in a dour tone.

His uncle waved his fingers at him. Acting was his

cue; his means of escape from a disagreeable situation, and he was going to give a fine performance if the boy would let him.

"Please introduce me," he said with emphasis, continuing to talk in French.

"It's my uncle—Sir George Dillingham—Mademoiselle Rose Vibert," said Alexis quietly.

Rose put up her chin and gave a laugh.

"Congratulations, sir. You have caught the burglars red-handed."

"You must excuse my appearing like this," said Sir George. "May I come in?" For he was still standing outside the french window and Alexis blocked his way. Alexis silently moved aside and Sir George stepped into the room and immediately asked:

"How do you come to be rehearsing that charming little play—for it was a scene from—what's the name of it—by Mérimée that I overheard, wasn't it? Your tone and accent were quite excellent, Alexis. It was a moment before I recognised you."

"Charming of you to have come all the way from Paris to congratulate me," Alexis remarked as though addressing nobody in particular.

Sir George laughed, but it seemed that his stream of congratulations had run dry.

To the surprise of Alexis, Rose replied to his uncle: "I am so glad you appreciate him. As an actress I am very proud of my pupil. If he should be in want of a job I would recommend him to my director, who might find a small part for him in *The Master Builder*."

"Have you been acting in *The Master Builder?*" asked Sir George, without the slightest tone of surprise.

"I play the young girl, Hilda Wangel: the Rising Generation," said Rose.

"That interests me immensely. Because you have a most difficult problem. The last time I saw it, I realised the play was pure Freudian symbolism. It seemed inexpressibly ludicrous to hear the young girl apostrophising a symbolical erection ... and the whole theme turns on the Master Builder's sexual impotence. What was artistically perfect when the audience was unconscious of the symbolism, becomes comically crude. Can that very tricky problem ever be overcome?"

Alexis listened with contempt and astonishment to this speech of his uncle's. He was disgusted that such were the thoughts of a man who called himself a poet when listening to one of the great plays of the world. The ideas Sir George was putting forward were new to him and extremely antipathetic. Alexis had never read Freud or heard his ideas discussed. It was thus with extreme surprise that he heard Rose saying:

"That is exactly how one or two of our company felt when we first read the play together and discussed it before the rehearsals began. Marcel, our chief, who acts the Master Builder, maintained that it didn't matter. He pointed out that you get the same phallic symbolism in religious ceremonies. We can admire the spire of a church, or watch a finger being inserted into a ring during a marriage ceremony without giggling. Marcel would say that when you saw *The Master Builder*, just after reading Freud for the first time, you were in the condition of a schoolboy still upset by the discovery of puberty."

Rose's tone was caustic, but Sir George nodded his head in agreement.

Suddenly Rose burst into a warm, rich laugh.

"But I am being very rude indeed."

"Not in the least. I am half inclined to agree. I most certainly hope you are right and that a great work of art has not been spoilt by a discovery in science."

"Well, now you must excuse me," said Rose. "I will change my dress for something more appropriate. *Chéri*, will you give your uncle an aperitif? And do take off your cassock. It makes you seem so censorious."

Sir George gave an appreciative laugh and remained looking after her when she had left the room.

"Well, Mademoiselle Vibert has answered most of the questions I came to ask," he remarked, speaking for the first time in English.

"What did old Jerôme tell you?" asked Alexis, still in the same dour tone of voice.

"The poor old fellow was most terribly worried . . . so I thought out of common humanity I must come down and put things straight," said Sir George airily.

"I have a lot to explain and now that you are here there is something I wish to ask you," said Alexis in as reasonable a tone of voice as he could manage.

"By all means, my dear fellow. But do get rid of that *soutane* and give me a drink first."

The clerical disguise suited Alexis's mood and he was loath to take it off. However, he pulled it over his head, and then in his shirt sleeves went out of the room.

Left alone, Sir George threw up his arms and exclaimed:

"*Tableau!* But what a girl!"

Alexis reappeared carrying three glasses and hugging bottles.

"Chambéry vermouth, white wine, or *porto?*" he asked. "*Porto* is what Rose drinks."

"Chambéry please." Alexis filled a glass and gave it him and filled a glass of white *Gaillac* wine for himself.

"Now, my dear fellow, do tell me how it all started," his uncle asked him in the most cajoling tone and then suddenly added: "By the way—to prevent any misunderstanding—I ought to tell you that I've booked a room for myself at the *Hôtel de France*. I don't want to be *de trop*. I shall take myself off after supper."

Alexis stared at him for a moment and then in a very different voice said: "Rose was playing Hedda in Montpellier. I went every night. The play flopped, leaving her stranded with no money. I introduced myself and suggested our coming here till the company she's in opens at Albi next week."

As his uncle said nothing, he went on:

"I didn't expect to have to face the music until after she had gone. I thought I would ask you to charge what rent you thought reasonable and take it out of my allowance."

"That's absurd . . . but since you insist on talking about money, the thing that worried old Jerôme was your running up bills."

"Not very large ones. I should think it would amount to about ten or twelve thousand for the full fortnight, apart from the electricity. Rose and I may be able to pay most of that between us."

"Don't speak of it again. You haven't lost your sense of the value of money. But seriously, I must congratulate you from the little I have seen of Mademoiselle Rose."

Alexis smiled. "It's very nice of you to say that." Then his face hardened.

"What I really wanted to ask you was not to do with the money part of it—but to let Rose stay on here until she's due to go to Albi. She has less than three thousand francs and nowhere to go. If you turn her out she will have to get a lodging in a ghastly slum and will starve herself."

The boy's voice, which had been matter-of-fact in telling his story, shook with passion and he seemed unable to go on.

"My dear boy . . . my dear fellow. Of course I should not dream of doing anything of the kind." Sir George sounded hurt.

"Well, I suppose that's what you came down from Paris to do," said Alexis. "However, if you are not going to, it's all right and thank you very much indeed. If you'll excuse me, I'll tell Rose what you've said and dish up the dinner." Without waiting for a reply he left the room.

Sir George filled his glass, emptied it and filled it again while the sound of a rapid conversation came from the staircase.

"I tell you that I shall," he could hear Rose call out in loud emphatic tones.

In the ten minutes which followed, Sir George had time to wonder whether he had not made a fool of himself.

"Not for the first time, either."

However, it would not have been possible to turn them out—and he could still tell Alexis that this must be the last escapade of its kind. Yes, he would make that crystal clear.

At last the door opened and the young woman whom he had seen in a petticoat and a Spanish shawl was standing in the threshold in a white and silver lamé evening dress which Lady Dillingham had once worn at a ball given by Lady Cunard. Her hair, her colouring and her figure were not unlike Delia's forty years ago. Sir George stared at her for a few minutes without comprehension; he suddenly felt older; his eyes dazzled and his lips quivered. A fume of anger and of faintness left him feeling weak; he felt for a chair and sat down. In the distance he heard Mademoiselle Vibert saying: "I have some confessions to make . . ." But he spoke, not to her, but to Alexis, in a hurried aside:

"I say, my boy, fetch the flask out of the dash-pocket in my car." Alexis looked at his uncle and went quickly.

When he came back Rose was kneeling beside Sir George, who was patting her on the shoulder and saying: "Of course, of course, why shouldn't you wear it, my dear? You are beautiful enough. Please forgive this performance. My heart doesn't often play me these tricks. I'm all right now." He poured himself a wineglass of brandy and drank it and the colour came back rapidly into his grey cheeks.

A few minutes later they were sitting at table, and while they ate, Sir George began talking. It was at once apparent that talking was an art at which he excelled and that it was no handicap to him to be talking in a language which was not his own. His voice was beautiful; his accent faintly English and aristocratic; but there was a personal warmth, a friendliness that was the man himself. Like most elderly men he spoke of the past—which for his hearers was the distant past, but for him a world only of yesterday which he could scarcely believe had vanished.

Alexis learned that evening that the famous actress who had married his uncle had been married before she met him and that her first husband had refused to give her a divorce. She had fallen in love with Sir

George before the first war when he was a young officer and they had gone away together after it was over to live the rest of their lives in France, though it had meant her giving up the stage.

"I had always wanted to be a poet. She took up painting. Naturally we saw a lot of artists, writers and stage people." Diaghilev, Copeau, Marcel Proust, Maxine Eliot, Isadora Duncan, Gertrude Stein, Marie Laurencin, Antoine Bibesco, Paul Valéry: a string of names, all living individuals in his mind, but invested with the glamour of a dead world to his listeners, were sprinkled through his stories.

Rose learned that Delia had died in the spring of 1940 and that a lucky chance had taken him back to England a few weeks before the French collapsed. He had remained throughout the war working as a liaison officer with the Free French.

An hour later, drinking a third cup of coffee, he was saying to Rose: "I'm very glad Alexis invited you to come and stay here, my dear. And I'm very glad I came down to see for myself . . . Of course you must stay here until you go to Albi. I shall see if I can turn up to see you in *The Master Builder*—or in that little curtain-raiser of Mérimée's. Well, now I must be off to my hotel. I've had a tiring day, what with one thing and another."

He gave Rose a kiss on the cheek and a pat on the shoulder. "God bless you, my dear. *Au revoir.*"

Alexis went with his uncle to his car.

"I wish I had had your character when I was your

age. I congratulate you on falling in love with Rose. It makes me feel that I understand you so very much better. You have always been a bit of a dark horse." Sir George pulled out his pocket-book and, taking out four five-thousand franc notes, gave them to Alexis.

"When you want some more, let me know. You may want to give her some little keepsake. I'll pay for the groceries, of course, and I'll square old Jerôme tomorrow morning. You stay here till the fortnight is up. But then you really ought to go back to work, don't you think? You are a bit young to spend your time following Mademoiselle Vibert round France. You must try and look on it as an interlude. You'll never forget it."

Then, when he was seated in the car and had started the engine, he added in French:

"Ce sera un souvenir léger pour toi."

He let in the clutch and the old Rolls moved away silently. Alexis watched it with a curious smile on his lips until the tail lights were hidden by a bend in the road.

"So near and yet so far," he said to himself. "I wonder whether I shall be so generous and warm when I am his age—and then 'a little keepsake.' How absurdly Edwardian!" He shrugged his shoulders and walked back into the villa.

Rose was walking up and down the drawing-room in passionate agitation. Alexis saw, to his astonishment, that she was actually wringing her hands.

"What am I to do? I can never forgive myself, I

am an unimaginative bitch, a madwoman, a brute, vulgar, common, horrible. Why didn't you stop me wearing that dress?" Rose suddenly demanded, turning angrily on Alexis.

"But my darling, he didn't mind, after the first moment of shock. I did tell you I thought it was a bit risky. But it turned out to be an enormous success."

"Risky! Who cares for that? Can't you see I made myself so cheap, so common, a strumpet dressed up in his dead wife's clothes? Why didn't you tell me he was like that? You should have explained. You should have stopped me by force. How could I tell that you should have a man like that for your uncle?"

Alexis for the first time felt exasperated with Rose: he had warned her not to dress up, but she had insisted on doing so and was now blaming him for having allowed it. However, he controlled his feelings, put his arm round her and kissed her and said:

"My uncle adores you. He gave me twenty thousand francs to pay for our holiday and told me to ask him for more to buy you a keepsake."

"You see, he thinks I am a common tart that you picked up in Montpellier."

"Don't be absurd. He congratulated me on falling in love with you and said that meeting you had made him understand me for the first time."

Little by little Rose allowed herself to be comforted and they went to bed. But, by the time she had uttered the last sigh of satisfaction, Alexis was feeling exasperated again with hearing his uncle's praises.

"Damn him for coming and upsetting everything," he said to himself before he finally fell asleep. Certainly if Rose had brought nephew and uncle closer together, the latter had not had the same effect upon the pair of lovers. Next day Rose was unsettled and Alexis felt ill-used; the unclouded weather of their love was gone. Rose was at moments passionate and then would suddenly burst out laughing at Alexis unkindly, or reproaching him. Then, in the twinkling of an eye, she would hit herself on the head and declare that Alexis was an angel of goodness. It was all her fault. She was a selfish creature and a bad character.

Alexis could not imagine what possessed her, but he made up his mind that another such day would be unendurable. Something must be done. In the afternoon Rose disappeared without telling him, and when he was becoming anxious, came back saying she had been into the town to go to a cinema.

Next morning Alexis took Rose a cup of early coffee while she was still in bed, still half-asleep, and said:

"Get up, we are going for an excursion."

"What do you mean, darling?" asked Rose, sitting bolt upright.

"We are taking the bus to Gavarnie to see the Pyrenees."

"See the Pyrenees! But we can see them very well out of the window."

"You are going to see them from the back of a horse."

"When did you decide this, Oh Lord and Master?"

"Yesterday, when you told me I was an unimaginative boy."

"Darling, I am horrible. I don't deserve such goodness . . . but are we really going to ride horses?"

"Possibly they will be mules."

"Then I must wear trousers. I will be ready in five minutes."

That day's excursion brought great happiness, but when Alexis looked back on it, its events were mixed up and fragmentary: he could not dwell on them.

They had had to wait in the main street of Lourdes for another bus. The main street seemed to him like a huge Woolworth bazaar full of junk, and then Alexis had the delightful surprise of discovering that Rose disliked Lourdes as much as he did. From the bus they saw vivid scenes of forest foothills: green strips of level pasture dotted with heavy cattle and the spruces rising and hiding all from view; a rocky trout stream; a ruined tower crowning a rock, the first of the high mountains close, white with snow; men hauling logs with a team of oxen, the shrill whine of a circular saw near the road, heard above the rattle of the bus, ancient farmhouses with thick fortified walls rising from the brilliant green turf. A wait in a little village with an ancient church followed and then they came to Gavarnie itself, with the great wall of mountains hemming them in.

At the top of the little village street a boy with two

horses was waiting as though he had known that they were coming.

Rose and he were both delighted with their own ability. Each of them swung into the saddle without help and found the other stirrup instantly. They scrambled over a rocky path, Alexis leading the way and Rose talking to the boy behind him. Up and down, down and up, and at last out upon a level stretch of beaten earth beside a mountain stream. They had come to the *Cirque des Pyrénées*.

The mountains were all round them, immense and inaccessible, and far up was a square gap in the cliff face where Oliver and Roland had held the Saracens from crossing into France. Only—it was incredible that any army could have climbed to such remote heights among the snow.

They turned their horses and rode back, their guide sometimes urging their ancient lean mounts into a faltering trot. Then, cautiously they slid and picked their way among the sharp rocks. "Marvellous!" Each was relieved to be once more on *terra firma* and they walked down the main street of Gavarnie well content with the way they had come out of a difficult situation.

"Where did you learn to ride?" asked Alexis.

"On the wooden horses in the Luxembourg gardens," replied Rose, in a matter-of-fact tone. It was the only remark of hers made during the excursion that he afterwards remembered and yet he had the feeling that she had talked a lot. They ate with enormous relish and on the way home Rose dozed off, and to steady her, Alexis put his arm round her. Her full breast was pressed on to his chest, her head of dark rusty tangled hair lay against his neck and on his shoulder. From the moment they had got into the bus until their return, neither of them thought once of Sir George Dillingham.

When they reached the door of *Les Pervenches*, Rose turned to Alexis and said: "Before you come in, pick me some chives and a sprig of thyme. I'll cook the supper: I'll make you a Basque omelette in honour of our outing."

"I don't think we've enough eggs," said Alexis.

"Go and get some chives all the same," said Rose.

"All right; in a minute," and Alexis unlocked the door.

On the mat he saw lying a pale blue piece of paper: a telegram. He picked it up and handed it to Rose, on whose face he saw a curiously desperate expression. She opened it and said:

"It's from Marcel. He wants me at Albi at once. Utter nonsense."

Alexis did not reply but went into the garden. A few minutes later he returned. "Here are your chives," he said, putting them on the dresser.

Rose began to laugh rather hysterically and flung her arms round him.

"I need not go. I'm sure it's all nonsense."

"Don't talk like that. Of course you will go. Your work must come first. I could not endure it if I knew you ought to be working and were staying for my sake."

Later that evening, when she repeated that she was not going to Albi, Alexis got really angry.

"You know that you have got to go and it is heartless to pretend that you will stay. Not that your love for me is a pretence," he added reflectively. "Anyone can see what your love has done for me in a few days. It is obvious. But I have done something for you also. When you play Juliet you'll know how to act her all the better because you have loved me. And so I shall have a share in your success as well as Marcel and the men who taught and trained you."

They were lying side by side with the light on. Rose sat up in bed, looked at him, turned away and burst into sobs.

"Not Juliet; Cressida or Manon. I'm so unhappy and I deserve to be. Come, darling." Her tears flowed silently for some time after she had ceased sobbing, and as he kissed her he discovered that the salt taste of them was delicious and singularly gratifying. At last they stopped flowing and Rose lay without movement as he comforted her with love.

She went the next morning by the early train. Alexis stayed on at the villa till the afternoon to tidy up the house, put away books and dresses and settle up with old Jerôme.

In the kitchen he found the crumpled telegram. It had been dispatched, not from Albi, but from Paris.

"I wonder how he can have known Rose's address.

I feel sure she never wrote any letters," he said aloud, and as the question stayed in his mind unanswered, another idea came to him, when he noticed the withered chives lying on the dresser.

"She wanted to hide something. If I had gone and picked them when she asked me, she would still be here. She knew the telegram was waiting for her, inside the door. She must have asked him to send it. 'Not Juliet—but Manon or Cressida.' It makes sense only if she telegraphed to Marcel to send it when she went out the day before. And then she changed her mind coming home in the bus. And I forced her to go and she dared not confess her plot to get away from me. That makes sense. I don't suppose I shall ever know for certain. Not that the details matter a damn. And all to get away three days before she had to go anyway."

Alexis returned to Montpellier by a night train. He looked very old and tired, and the *patronne* of the pension where he boarded, who had meant to make jokes about his disappearance, shut her mouth with a snap and ten minutes later went to his room with a bowl of soup into which she had put a tablespoonful of marsala.

Part Two

Alexis did not go to see Rose at Albi, and though he wrote to her several times, she did not reply. Living in France, he was reminded of her at every moment and he decided that his existence had become unendurable. He therefore returned to England and wrote to Sir George that he had arranged to do his military service immediately.

Two years later Alexis was a Captain in a Parachute Battalion returning from Malaya. The troopship in which he was travelling put in at Marseilles and his Colonel gave him permission to return to England overland. One of his recurrent day-dreams, when he had been fighting in the jungle, had been arriving at Paris to find Rose's face placarded on the hoardings outside a theatre, watching the play, and walking into her dressing-room after the performance. Every time he allowed himself the luxury of that day-dream he said to himself: "First she will fall into my arms and kiss me and then she will introduce me to her husband." Nevertheless, he did not quite believe that the husband would count for much, even if he existed.

Now he was going to translate the dream into reality, for his object in visiting Paris was to see if he could find Rose. It was possible that if she had continued on the stage and made a name for herself, his uncle might be able to tell him where to find her. If she had left the stage, which he thought very improbable, it would be more difficult and he would have to wait until he had been demobilised.

Alexis got off the train at the *Gare de Lyon*, took a taxi and drove to the *Île St Louis* where Sir George Dillingham had a flat. He had stayed there for a few weeks before his uncle had sent him to study at Montpellier. When his taxi had crossed the bridge he stopped it, paid it off, and walked the last fifty yards to his uncle's door. It was a lovely morning and he wanted to enjoy his surroundings.

The island stood timeless in the heart of the whirling, changing, kaleidoscopic city, the busy highway of the river hemming it in on each side. It was inhabited, it was not set apart—a memory of Trinity Great Court and of a Temple in Ceylon flashed into his mind. It was not like such places for it was a living part of Paris—and yet it was timeless and enchanted so that to be on the island was to be in two worlds at once: the world of Paris and the world of a fairy story. And yet, for all that, it was slovenly and humdrum.

With these reflections in his mind, Alexis pressed the button, walked into the hall and entered the lift that took him up to his uncle's flat. It was only half-past eight when he rang the bell, but he supposed that Sir George would be awake and would give him breakfast.

An old woman, whom he supposed he had seen before, opened the door and at once exclaimed:

"Ah! How you have grown, Monsieur Alexis. And in uniform! Come in. Let me take your bag." He stepped into the hall and had shut the door before she added: "Sir George is away on a little visit to Venice. But I will tell Madame."

"Madame?" Alexis hesitated. It would be better for him to go away at once, but he didn't like to be brusque with the old woman, whose name he had just remembered was Elizabeth. She was asking him if he would like an English breakfast with bacon and a fried egg and English marmalade.

"Just give it me in the kitchen—and don't tell Madame," he said.

"Ah! That is like you. But Madame would be terribly disappointed not to see you." And Elizabeth, carrying his hold-all, went out, leaving him in the dining-room.

"Extraordinary of Uncle George to marry again after all these years, but it would be silly to feel self-conscious, whoever she may be," Alexis said to himself. The room was, as he had remembered it, the most beautiful that he had ever been in. It was slightly asymmetrical with two great windows looking out over the end of the island and down the Seine. And if you got tired of the view of Paris, there was the big Cézanne, the Matisse and the Berthe Morisot on the stained and rather shabby walls.

He had turned back to look out of the window again when someone opened the door. Rose called out his name and as he turned she came quickly to him and put her arms on his shoulders and kissed him. His lips were on her cheek when the realisation came that she was Madame.

He stepped back and had a look at her. She was changed very little. She was more beautiful than he remembered. Much more beautiful. Exquisitely clean and *soignée*—wearing a close-fitting jersey of black and white wool and a checked skirt.

"Darling, this is wonderful," she said, and then stopped short, seeing his expression.

Alexis tried to laugh but only succeeded in giving a grin.

"The most beautiful room in the world," he said. "And Uncle George certainly has a talent for collecting lovely objects ... I am right in supposing that you are one of them?"

Rose did not reply.

"Have you married him?" asked Alexis.

"No."

"Why not?"

"There is no question of marriage between George and me."

"Wouldn't you like to be Lady Dillingham?"

"Why do you take this tone with me, Alexis?"

He turned away from her and looked out of the window. There was a barge coming up-stream and a man, a woman and a little girl with pigtails were sitting on deck eating breakfast. It was a Dutch barge.

Alexis turned back to where Rose was standing, silent and very pale.

"Because I like to see things clearly. You have hidden this relationship for two years and I have only just discovered it. The moment you met my uncle, you threw me over for his money. That is why you sent yourself that telegram at Pau."

"That is not true." For the second time he noticed that she was wringing her hands. Alexis watched the movement and wondered whether it was natural or a stage trick that she had cultivated.

At last she said: "I detest scenes and theatricalities. Because we loved each other and enjoyed an idyll for a fortnight, you cross-examine me and accuse me. Why cannot you look at life and try to understand it?"

"I think I do understand it and see it as it is," replied Alexis.

At first his voice sounded dull and almost dead. But as he went on his tone became heated and passionately indignant.

"It is simple enough. You were starving and poor.

I could only offer you an idyll and a roof over your head for a fortnight, a roof that did not even belong to me. My uncle could offer you luxuries, could push you in your profession perhaps. And, as you said once yourself, you are Manon, not Juliet. My uncle had the resources to buy you. I had not. But at least admit that he did buy you. For I believe you loved me at Pau."

"Of course I did. You were enchanting. I may even love you now, though you are stupid and horrible."

"Yet you threw me over instantly. You could not wait three days, simply because my uncle was a good business proposition."

"Listen, Alexis. Being in the army has not improved your intelligence. You talk of George's money. Of course he does give me material objects. Why not? But the reasons why I am living with him are not material. What he has given me is far more precious than this bracelet, or this string of pearls. Living with him in this room has been an education."

"I'm sure of it," interjected Alexis in a tone of extreme irony, but Rose took no notice of the remark and continued:

"He has made me enter into the past. Through him I have learned to understand the generation which knew Sarah and Duse and Proust and Gide. George has a fascination that no boy of your age could offer. I owe it entirely to George that I am almost free of the traditional vices of the ordinary actress. He has taught me to look at myself impartially."

Rose suddenly threw herself down in an armchair with a movement of utter exhaustion.

"So you threw over love for culture and education—not simply for money?" said Alexis.

"But I love George. I left you at Pau because I had fallen in love with him—I got Marcel to send me that telegram, not knowing whether I should ever see George again."

"You pretend that you prefer him to me for himself?" asked Alexis with a touch of interest in his voice.

"I don't compare you. But, if you insist, I do prefer him. He isn't an egoist. He doesn't bully, or try and dominate me, or make scenes. He is kind, and for him loving means being kind."

"So all that, added up, enables you to put up with him physically as a lover?"

Rose stared at Alexis in such astonishment that he wondered if her emotion could be genuine.

"But I love him. And he makes love perfectly. Even better than you did. He is by no means impotent, if you want to know."

Alexis's face set like a stone. What she had said could only be to wound him. He walked towards her suddenly with a murderous expression on his face and stood over her where she sat motionless.

"What a nasty little bitch you are; trying to hurt me by a lie of that sort. I have loved you for two long years. I dreamed of you every night in the jungle. And I only came here this morning to see if my uncle had a clue as to where you were, or knew what had happened to you. I wonder I don't kill you. I've got a pistol in my pocket and I might just as well shoot you as not."

Rose looked at him with an expression of despair and shrugged her shoulders. She made no other movement and sat silent, searching his face for some sign that did not appear.

At last she said: "Even if you have been in the jungle for years, try to use your intelligence. Don't make a scene but talk sensibly as you used to do. You *must* understand. George is not some sort of satyr because he is sixty-four years old. He is infinitely amusing and sympathetic. I love him more than any man I have ever known in my life. I am deeply grateful to him for loving me—and I am not lying when I say that he makes love enchantingly. Don't look so disgusted, as though you would like to be sick. Don't let jealousy make you idiotic. I beg you not to bolster up your *amour propre* with an illusion of George as an old orang-outang buying the body of a gold-digging harlot."

Rose paused for a moment and then said with extreme ferocity:

"And before you threaten me again, please understand who you are speaking to: I earn quite enough money already not to need anyone else's. I could have any one of a score of lovers, if I wished. I am on the way to becoming famous and men find me attractive. Lots of them are far richer than George.

Yet I have been faithful to him for over a year; more faithful to him than he is to me."

Suddenly her eyes filled with tears which she brushed away angrily. She had not meant to speak of George's visit to Giulietta, or to think of it.

Alexis left her and went to the window again. The Dutch barge had disappeared. Although it was so early in the morning, a pair of lovers were standing under the trees below, looking out over the river. At last he turned towards her and she could see that there were tears on his cheeks and in his eyes.

"I'll go away now," he said. "Try and forgive me if you can. But it was a shock."

"You will *not* go away," said Rose standing up. "Just when I have found you. You will spend the day here until I have to go to the theatre. I'm playing rather an amusing part."

Alexis stood hesitating and stiff and Rose opened her arms and threw them around him. "Try and understand and it will not hurt so much."

Almost at once there was a little tap at the door and Elizabeth put her head in. "May I bring in Monsieur Alexis's breakfast?" she asked.

The rest of the morning they avoided talking of love. Alexis spoke of the army and of fighting the Chinese terrorists in the Malayan jungle, and Rose spoke of the parts she had played, of her triumphs and her failures and of how she was still with Marcel, who had at last got his own theatre in Paris.

Alexis had a bath and dressed himself in a suit of

Sir George's fluffy tweeds, although Rose declared that she would rather be accompanied by an officer in battledress with a claret-coloured béret and a couple of ribbons on his chest.

They went out and strolled across the bridge and made their way towards the flower market and Rose bought an immense bunch of yellow roses and sent them to a friend who had recently had a baby. When they came back Alexis was feeling as though the nightmare of the morning had never happened.

"Did I say all those things, or did we only dream them?" he said to her as they went up in the little lift.

"Oh. You are clever. You are escaping responsibility and trying to avoid your punishment. And you still have a pistol in your pocket ready to shoot me," said Rose.

Elizabeth had lunch ready for them: stewed fennel, saddle of lamb roasted with rosemary and new peas. They drank champagne.

"What are you going to give me for dessert?" asked Alexis insolently, looking at Rose.

She blushed deeply and seemed embarrassed. "So you remember that? I don't think you want ... Oh well, I'm not very happy just now. Fill your glass then and come into my room."

Alexis went to see Rose playing 'an amusing part'; they had supper together afterwards and about two o'clock in the morning he suddenly said: "But all this passion is a pretence, isn't it, like your wonderful performance this evening at the theatre? Because really you prefer Uncle George in bed."

"Be quiet," said Rose. "Don't talk about things you don't understand. However, if we must start again on this subject let me tell you something. There is one thing in your favour, darling. It is not what George doesn't give me, either physically or in any other way. He gives me infinitely more than you can. But I can give him very little. He lives a good deal out of my reach, in the past. With you I can make, at every moment, an impression that will last you the rest of your life. With him I am only the embers on the fire; I cannot produce a conflagration. All the same he does in a way depend on me. But nothing I said or did would make him want to shoot me."

Alexis suddenly said: "Oh, drop the subject, please. I won't mention him again if you will promise not to."

"There is one thing I want to ask you about him before I promise," said Rose. "Tell me truthfully, if you can, is he a good poet?"

"What does that matter?" said Alexis crossly.

"I would like to know your opinion, anyway. I can understand very little English, but I try to read his poems and have even learned one of them by heart. I imagine that he is, but I can't tell."

"Well, I think in a way, he is," replied Alexis. "His poetry does not interest me. It is curiously flat, without verbal richness or grandeur, or any attempt at wit. And it is not at all technically exciting. But in his flat way he does seem to be able to deal with delicate and complex emotions, and to be able to reduce them to manageable proportions. Rather like reflecting the moon in a bucket of water. That's a good comparison, for his poetry is rather Chinese. Waley has influenced him more than Eliot, or the younger men."

"He has written some poems about me," said Rose. "Rather intimate. I will show you them tomorrow."

"Damn you. You are a bitch, as I have already said once today. I don't want to read them."

"All right, I will not mention them again," said Rose. "You can show me your medals instead."

Alexis burst into a full-throated roar of laughter. "Darling, you certainly can give as good as you get."

Rose laughed happily. "Do you know how nice you are? I have never met any man except you and George who will laugh at a joke at his own expense. Now go and get that half-bottle of champagne that I put in the refrigerator after supper. I should like one glass and then I must go to sleep. I'm tired out after a day in the jungle."

They drank a glass of the pale wine and then Alexis finished the half-bottle. It was delicious and cold. "Light as the story of *A Midsummer Night's Dream*," said Alexis, who had drunk a little more at supper than he had imagined.

Rose was almost asleep when he asked: "But what will Elizabeth think if she finds me in bed with you in the morning?"

"Don't bother me with nonsense," murmured Rose sleepily.

Alexis spent three more days in Paris. On the last of them, a Sunday, when Rose was not giving a performance, she drove him, in Sir George's old Rolls, to Chartres. They spent an hour in the Cathedral and came home by Maintenon where they looked over the Château. Though Alexis was living in his uncle's flat, wearing his clothes, sleeping with his mistress and being driven in his car, he managed to avoid thinking about him for twenty-four hours. On Monday morning Rose received a letter from Italy and read it at breakfast with such intense eagerness that Alexis, watching her, realised she had forgotten he was in the room, or that he existed. When at last she looked up and spoke, her voice was calm and matter of fact. After breakfast she drove him to Le Bourget to take a plane for London and it came to him as a violent shock, after he had said gaily: "I shall be back in three weeks," to hear her reply:

"I don't want you to come back. George will be here then. Things will be different."

"What do you mean by that?" asked Alexis.

"Well, I shall be different," she replied. "I shan't want you then!" and she walked out of the waiting room.

Rose was waiting when the express from Italy came in at the *Gare de l'Est* at 7.30 in the morning.

Sir George Dillingham had aged in the last two years: he had his ups and downs and Rose was afraid that after a night in the *wagons-lits* he would be feeling a little sorry for himself. But he held himself erect as he got out.

They embraced warmly and the innocent blue eyes crinkled up with pleasure.

"I thought I would meet you and I've brought the car."

"Darling, I had a wild hope that you would meet me, but I didn't expect it."

A porter put Sir George's bag in the boot and then, to Rose's relief, George walked round and got into the driving seat. That was a good sign, for when he was indulging in self-pity, or feeling depressed about his age, he made Rose drive. Usually he drove himself. Thus, although Rose greatly enjoyed driving the Rolls and being seen driving it, on this occasion she preferred not to be allowed to do so.

After a little while George said: "So you've been having company. Of course I can't complain as I went off to stay with Giulietta!"

Rose said nothing. George did some rather intricate steering and then asked: "What's the fellow like? I suppose you've fallen in love with him again?"

"At first I thought he was quite changed. It was partly the effect of the uniform and the military manner, and the little moustache. He had become rather vain; rather pig-headed; a little stupid. But physically he's just as attractive as he used to be."

"I rather gathered that from your letter. But how did the bad qualities you mention show themselves?"

Rose shrugged her shoulders. "It is difficult to explain. His whole tone was idiotic. He even threatened to shoot me at one moment. Can you imagine anything so stupid?"

"Oh, I say! Poor chap. You must have been an awful bitch to drive him to that."

"That's just what he called me. Of course you would sympathise with him if he had actually murdered me and you found me lying in a pool of blood, wouldn't you, darling?"

Elizabeth had some hot coffee, fresh *croissants* and butter waiting, and stayed and gossiped while they breakfasted. Then George went to the bathroom, and he was lying soaking in the hot water when Rose came in.

"You have got brown in Italy," she exclaimed, and sat down to talk.

After a while, George asked: "When is he coming back?"

"I hope never. But actually he said he would come back in two or three weeks. I told him you would be back and I should not want him. I have quite made up my mind to send him packing."

George said nothing.

"I refuse to be forced into an emotional crisis. My work will suffer terribly. I have no real feeling for him. Of course I feel a little sentimental about him. And I must admit—he excites me. But I love you and I am happy with you."

"Oh, leave me out."

"No, I won't leave you out. You know perfectly well that I can't stand young men. They are all shy, self-conscious and clumsy when they make love— and when they aren't making love they are arrogant and domineering. Whereas you . . ."

"My dear, if you talk to me about that sort of thing I shall get out of the bath and make you soaking wet . . . Why have you got that hat on?"

"I promised to go to Marcel's and have a drink before lunch. He needs my support. M. Sartre is going to be there."

"So on the very first day I am to be left to have lunch alone."

"I shall be back by half-past one."

"That means half-past two. The food will be spoilt. Elizabeth will be furious and I shall be sick with hunger."

"Really you are a spoilt child, George."

"I was only trying to prove how young I am—by domineering."

Rose laughed and then leant over and kissed his wet brown body floating in the water. "You taste of soap," she said, making a face.

"Shall I splash your new hat?"

"You dare!" She went off quickly. All was well. She had avoided betraying her jealousy of the Italian woman. She and George were on happy terms as though nothing had happened, and while she drove herself to the other end of Paris, attracting a lot of attention and enjoying doing so, he got out of the bath, dried himself on a warm towel, put on a dressing-gown and began to read his letters.

It was already dark when the Air France plane circled Le Bourget and the lanes of light that were the runways seemed disconcertingly hemmed in by the patchy and curly lights of buildings and streets. Alexis had lived for a few months among unforeseen and deadly dangers, but not long enough to have become seriously apprehensive of them. He was still a brave man with a taste for danger and tonight he was seeking one of his own creation, and was feeling once again the sensation of being an automaton, carried to its destiny by irrevocable decrees. It was the familiar sensation of impending battle or ambush. He put his hand in his pocket and felt a smooth lump of metal.

Neatly folded in his waistcoat pocket was a telegram:

"Do not on any account come to Paris. You are not wanted. Rose."

Alexis had argued to himself, in London, that its very violence showed fear and spoke in his favour. He had decided that he must, by whatever ruthless methods, eliminate George and then carry Rose by storm. One thing was certain. He would go all lengths. He had made up his mind that he would not live without her.

For weeks he had been living in solitude as though London were as empty as the Sahara. Alexis had no friends except those he had made in the Army—now demobilised and dispersed—and two or three young men in Montpellier whom he was unlikely ever to meet again. His secret emotional life was entirely wrapped up in thoughts of Rose and George.

The plane banked and the pilot throttled back.

"Here I jump," occurred to him and for a moment the thought of the danger and bewilderment of the jump would have been welcome. It would be fitting to descend on Paris from the dark and lonely spaces of the air. Instead of which there was the moment's tension of the run in, touching and bumping and dashing faster than an express train through the darkness.

Three-quarters of an hour later, at half-past eleven, he was ringing the bell of the flat on the island of St. Louis. Elizabeth opened the door. "Ah, Monsieur Alexis! I had almost given up expecting you."

Her words surprised him. He said nothing; his face expressionless.

"So you are no longer a soldier?"

"I still feel like one," he said, making an effort to smile.

"But you do not obey orders," said Elizabeth.

Alexis looked at her incredulously and with horror. So Rose made everything public: the old woman knew why he had come and she wanted to put her word in. It was insufferable.

"Quite right," he replied. "I don't obey orders. I give them. Is Mademoiselle Rose in?"

"Madame has not yet returned from the theatre."

"And my uncle?"

"Sir George went to the performance also."

When Elizabeth went out Alexis walked up and down the room feverishly and looked out of the window. Under the lamp a pair of lovers were embracing: the girl seemed in a state of catalepsy. Another pair made a dark outline leaning over the parapet.

Elizabeth came back with a tray: cold ham, salad, cold asparagus and mayonnaise and half a bottle of white wine. Alexis was hungry: he had not eaten since breakfast, but he had to force himself to eat and drink and soon got up and began walking about again.

Elizabeth came on him in the passage soon afterwards looking up a number in the telephone book.

"They will have left the theatre long ago," she said.

Alexis did not reply but shut the book and went back into the dining-room and sat down to wait with his head in his hands. Half an hour later the telephone rang. He dashed into the passage, but Elizabeth was putting the receiver on its hook.

"Who was that?" he asked.

"Madame rang up to ask if you were here."

"Where did she ring from?"

"I have no idea."

Alexis went back into the dining-room. It was one o'clock.

About three hours later he took his .32 Webley automatic out of his pocket and laid it on the table.

"If she comes in now I shall shoot her," he whispered. And then almost immediately added: "Am I mad or sane? Do I feel what I imagine I feel, or am I an automaton?" He became aware that he was in pain and had been in pain for some time past and that he was grinding his teeth.

He felt ashamed of doing so and at once stopped.

"*Je m'en fous de la psychologie*," he said aloud.

He had forgotten to put his pistol back into his pocket when Elizabeth came into the room at half-past seven with a tray on which there was hot coffee, *croissants*, curls of butter and a pot of Oxford marmalade.

"Do you mind moving your pistol?" she said, as there was not room on the small table for the tray. He remembered that he had not meant her to see it, as he put it away.

"Would you like to take a bath? I am sure you would find it refreshing," she said gently.

Alexis ate the breakfast, took the bath and shaved and felt as though an enormous weight had fallen from his shoulders.

He wondered whether perhaps his plan were not a terrible mistake after all. "I shall go to the theatre tonight," he thought; "and if her understudy is playing the part, I shall go back to England on the next plane. Honour will be satisfied ... all the same I cannot live without her."

To try and stop his thoughts, he took *Le Rouge et Le Noir* out of the shelf and began reading with interest. He had reached the third chapter when the door opened and Rose walked in.

She was looking and feeling as fresh as a daisy and she was extremely angry. Alexis noticed with a feeling of pain that she was wearing the same jersey and skirt in which he had seen her on his arrival in Paris three weeks before.

"What do you imagine you are doing, camping here?" she began in a quiet, conversational tone. "I don't want to see you now, or ever again. If I still felt any love for you, or physical attraction, you have destroyed it forever by your insufferable selfishness. No, don't dare say a word. If it hadn't been for George, I should have been waiting here to throw you into the street. You know his heart is weak. You think you can blackmail me because I am anxious about him. How dare you come here after my telegram?"

Alexis, who had listened in silence, had turned dead white and suddenly began trembling uncontrollably.

"I came here because I can't live without you. If I can't have you I shall kill you."

"I've heard that story before," said Rose, still speaking very quietly. "And really I don't care a damn if you do. You won't make me love you any more by shooting me. Not only do I detest little imbeciles who commit murder out of wounded sexual vanity, but I love someone else with all my heart. I love George and I wish you had never come back. You are so vain that you cannot understand that I do not love you. And you are such a bully and a coward that you think you can dominate me by violence."

As she spoke Alexis took his pistol out of his pocket. He was dead white and the hand in which he held it was shaking uncontrollably. Rose looked at him with an expression of supreme contempt. She was so enraged by the sight of the weapon that it did not occur to her to feel afraid. "I will mark him for this," were the words she found in her mind and she picked up a silver candlestick from the writing-table.

"Have you finished? Have you said everything?" asked Alexis, speaking with difficulty.

"No. I've only just begun. As I have told you George has a weak heart. I cannot expose him to scenes of this sort. I had therefore to drag him off to the theatre and insist on his coming to a hotel last night—because of you. But you are not going to play that trick twice. I shall finish with you. If you are going to shoot me, do it now. It is your last chance because unless you agree to get on the next plane for England I shall send for the police and give you in charge."

"Did you never love me?" Alexis asked. He was breathing in gasps, as though he had been sobbing, but his eyes were dry.

"I don't remember and I don't care. It has nothing to do with this intolerable and horrible scene."

"Manon or Cressida," said Alexis.

These words infuriated Rose, who remembered when she had used them of herself. She had been wanting to hit Alexis from the moment that he had produced his pistol. Now, taking careful aim, she threw the silver candlestick at him and at the same moment ducked violently. Everything happened in a flash. The candlestick hit Alexis full in the mouth, cutting his lip, and his pistol went off. Elizabeth rushed into the room and hit him on the arm with a hammer. He dropped the pistol, the old woman snatched it off the floor and ran out of the room. Alexis stood motionless. He saw that he had shot Rose in the arm above the elbow. His mouth was full of blood.

He went up at once to the picture by Berthe Morisot, took it off the wall and, pulling out a large knife, cut off the cord from which it had been hanging.

"Do you see what you've done?" asked Rose. "You idiot."

"Hold out your arm. I'll put on a tourniquet," said Alexis, spitting out a broken tooth. But first he had to pull Rose's jersey over her head. She was wearing a very transparent lace brassière and the sight of her small rosy nipples made him think: "I should never have seen them again if I hadn't done this," and a lump came into his throat. After the first sight of her breasts, he avoided looking at them. Elizabeth reappeared while he was winding the picture cord under her armpit.

"Fetch a sponge and some bandages." As the old woman goggled and hesitated, he said: "Tear up a pillow-case if you have nothing better."

A moment later she came back carrying a pillow, and while she sponged the blood from the wound, he tore the pillow-case into strips and then bandaged the arm. "Sit down and hold your arm up," he said.

Up till that moment Rose had said nothing and had done exactly what he told her to do. But now she said: "I can't."

"What do you mean, you can't?"

"I can't hold it up."

"Oh, well, I'll put it in a sling."

When he had finished she said quietly: "Now you had better go and wash your face and try and stop your mouth from bleeding. And Elizabeth—bring us a bottle of champagne and some glasses."

When Alexis returned from the bathroom, he heard the pop of the cork and saw Rose filling a glass, holding the bottle in her left hand.

"You aren't supposed to take alcohol after a wound," he said.

"Well, you drink it yourself then," said Rose. "You have been looking like death, all the time."

He had drunk half the glass when there was the sound of someone opening the door of the flat and Sir George walked in.

"What have you done with the picture?" he asked, noticing the blank space on the wall.

The next moment he saw that Rose was half undressed: that she was wounded, with a bandage stained with blood.

"Oh, my God. I thought something like this would happen. I rushed round from the Ritz as soon as I woke up and found you gone. Thank God it's no worse. It's all my fault. I've come to tell you both. I am entirely to blame. You young creatures belong to one another. I've told you a hundred times, Rose, and you must see it for yourself. I'm going to leave now. It's quite fantastic."

"Hold your tongue," cried Rose, losing her self-command for the first time.

"I won't, I have made up my mind. I've come to say goodbye. I'm off to Venice this afternoon." Sir George had an immense amount more to say, but at those words Rose went off in a faint.

Alexis and Elizabeth laid her on the floor, sponged her face and when she came to, carried her into the bedroom.

"You had better have some champagne after all," said Alexis, who was feeling rather faint himself.

"Let's have lunch, Elizabeth," said Rose when she had revived. "We all need some food. There's room for both of you to sit on the bed."

While they ate cold chicken and eggs in mayonnaise Sir George brought up his idea once more.

"Really it could not be better. Alexis has brought

the inevitable about by this scene. You'll get well. You'll make each other happy."

"I never want to see the cowardly little rat again," said Rose to George, and then turning to Alexis, said politely:

"I suppose I ought to thank you for being so clever about stopping the bleeding and bandaging my arm. We don't want any of this to get into the papers, so I shan't see a doctor."

"I think it will be all right. Flesh wounds usually heal without trouble. Have you any sedative pills?" Alexis asked his uncle.

"Codeine any good? There's an old bottle of Nembutal and Disprin of course."

"Give her one of each," said Alexis to Elizabeth. The old woman nodded her head knowingly.

The two men hovered in the doorway for a moment while Elizabeth drew the bedroom curtains. Then they went into the dining-room.

"I don't know how it happened, or what on earth possessed me," said Alexis. "I think it was the awful discrepancy between the dream and the reality. I have been living alone with the thought of her for two years. And then I found her again...."

"I know, my boy, I know. I am so terribly guilty. I can't go on. I am going to leave her now. I don't really make her happy. If she won't have you, she'll find someone else and I shan't feel I am wasting the best years of her life."

"You won't mind if I stay on here until she's well and we can decide what to do?" asked Alexis.

"No, of course you must. I could not leave her like this if you were not here to look after her. And I think if I go now she will accept my going. I must not allow her to sacrifice herself any longer. It's horrible really. It's unnatural: only you know, it doesn't feel as though it were."

Alexis said nothing while his uncle walked up and down in agitation, reproaching himself and breaking off a sentence in order to stare for a minute out of the window. If he said the wrong thing it might turn the old man the other way. He could feel the decision trembling in the balance.

"Well, I must put a few things together in a bag. Elizabeth knows my address in Venice and will forward letters. You must promise to write tomorrow and for the next few days to let me know how she is."

Before Sir George left he had a word with Elizabeth, who broke into a torrent of expostulations as they stood in the passage with his big suitcase beside him.

"My dear Elizabeth. Will you please do as you are asked?" said Sir George testily.

"I'll have no hand in it," said the old woman furiously and went into the kitchen, slamming the door.

"Let me carry your suitcase," said Alexis, and picking it up walked out to the lift.

When Sir George had settled himself in the driving-seat, he paused and gazed silently at his nephew, finding no words.

Alexis found the strain unendurable. Suddenly he said:

"Would you mind giving me your latchkey? That old woman may refuse to open the door to me."

Sir George looked at him grumpily, and reluctantly took a key wallet out of his pocket, took the key off and gave it him.

"Mind you write. And telephone if there's any danger."

"There can't be," said Alexis. "Goodbye."

He watched the Rolls slip out of sight, rocking a little on the cobble-stones. Then he walked to the parapet and looked at the Seine. A breath of fresh air would do him good while Rose slept. But he was very tired and after he had crossed the girder foot-bridge built by the Germans, he went and sat down in the gardens of Notre-Dame for an hour. His victory was so astonishing that he could only brood on it as a fact. It was too early to wonder about all the changes in his life that would come with it.

At a few minutes after four he let himself into the flat with the latchkey and walked confidently into the dining-room. He was astonished to see Rose, with a brilliant Spanish shawl draped round her, sitting in an armchair.

"You must go straight back to bed," he said.

"Oh, there you are. So you have persuaded George to leave me so that you can take his place," she began in the easy conversational voice which he had learned to be afraid of. "Did he leave a message? What did he say before he left?"

"Nothing much more than he had said before: that it was all his fault and that he did not make you happy and that he must stop you wasting the best years of your life. He made me promise to look after you."

"So you imagine you are going to look after me?" said Rose. "You astonish me. Now please listen, for I have something important to tell you. I have rung up Marcel and told him that if he does not hear from me by five o'clock that you have left for England, he is to come round with a *huissier* to take my sworn statement and a police inspector to arrest you. Of course if you prefer to drown yourself in the Seine, I shall be delighted."

Alexis tried to move, tried to speak, tried to break the hideous dream, but he stood rooted, silent, hypnotised.

"Elizabeth," Rose called in a loud voice. The old woman came into the room.

"Give Monsieur Alexis his pistol. Go on, do what I tell you."

The old woman hesitated, but she fumbled at the placket-hole of her long skirt and produced the pistol from a pocket.

"I have not unloaded it, Monsieur. I did not know how." Alexis took it from her and put it in his pocket.

"Rose, you don't mean what you say."

"You know that I do mean what I say. I never want to see you again. You can blow your brains out in the taxi, or in the aeroplane, or now at this minute. I shall be delighted, so long as you don't miss again. Make a better job of it this time."

She was standing and Alexis felt that he had never really seen her before. Her rage was so controlled, so magnificent, she was so lovely; the contempt on her face so overwhelming. He thought she had never looked so splendid on the stage. He had not a word to say.

"Come," said Elizabeth and put her hand gently on his arm and pushed him towards and through the door and shut it behind him.

He was standing in the passage. "Give me the key," she insisted. He gave it her and they went together into the lift. Elizabeth said nothing further. Her wrinkled old face told him nothing and he was grateful to her for not saying a word of goodbye. She stood watching his departure expressionlessly until she heard the click of the outside door shutting.

An hour later, Alexis was in the coach taking him to Le Bourget and Sir George was on the road heading towards Switzerland, the Dolomites and Venice. He pulled up beside the road and scribbled a few lines of poetry on the back of a prospectus. Then he drove on again, carefully and slowly.

There was a ring at the bell of the flat.

Rose was lying in bed and Elizabeth was sitting silently near her.

"Go and open the door. That will be Marcel."

The fat man came into the bedroom with his handkerchief in his hand.

"You will kill me if you go on leading a life like this," he said. "I can't stand the strain. You must put your work first and cut all this out. I tell you, I don't think I shall ever get over this afternoon."

"What about me?" said Rose, bursting out laughing. "Marcel, you are an inimitable comic actor. A real comic genius. You are quite unaware that it is I who have been shot, not you."

"In another month you will have forgotten all about it," said Marcel. *"Ce sera un souvenir léger pour toi."*

Rose shook her head. "I shall need a month's convalescence at least. Tomorrow I am going to Venice. I am not going to let George go off to that Italian woman."

Part Three

When, four days after leaving Paris, having greatly enjoyed his drive through Switzerland and the Dolomites, Sir George strolled into the hotel in St. Mark's Square in Venice, where he had stayed for so many years that he felt completely at home in it, the manager rushed out, making hissing noises—"just like a goose," thought Sir George. The big fat Italian actually laid hold of his sleeve and with an expression of supplication almost pushed him into his little office and immediately locked the door and laid a finger on his lips.

"Thank God you have arrived, Sir George. I have been almost out of my mind," he exclaimed. "The publicity would have been terrible . . . ruin for us all."

"What's it all in aid of?" asked Sir George, quite unmoved.

"Madame Vibert is here ... she arrived the night before last in delirium, a high fever ... She told the porter who carried her bags up that your nephew had shot her in the arm and that you had run away from her ... Luckily I recognised her voice in the bar ... I had to put her to bed at once, call in a doctor I know, who is the soul of discretion. Then I had to get my spiritual director to recommend a nun to look after her, a nun who could be trusted not to say a word to the newspaper reporters. Lots of nuns like a chance to be indiscreet ..."

"Do you mean to say that you have a spiritual director, Leonardo?" asked Sir George with real interest in his voice.

"Naturally I have a spiritual director since I have done well for myself and am getting on in years," replied the Italian testily. "But this is very important for you and Madame ... Do you understand that Madame might have died in this hotel and that I should have been ruined? No, there's no fear of that now ... The doctor says the crisis is over ... The press are everywhere—a man comes round every day to look at our arrivals. He has been asking all sorts of questions. Luigi, the porter, is a nice boy, but keeping his mouth shut may be expensive for me ... I had no idea when you would turn up.... I have been mad with anxiety."

"Don't exaggerate, Leonardo," said Sir George.

"Exaggerate! What do you think Madame was telling the barman? That she had come to Venice, that she had followed you here, to get you away from the Marchesa Trapani. She actually named her, in front of a crowd of people. Luckily they were Americans and she was talking French. How would that have looked in the American newspapers, I ask you? A *crime passionnel* and a drama of jealousy. What a scandal it would make!"

"Very trying for you. Well, I'll trot along and see how she is. But I must think seriously about getting myself a spiritual director: you know I'm a lot older than you are, Leonardo," and Sir George unlocked the office door and walked across to the lift.

The manager shook his fist at his back as he entered it.

"*Stupido!*" he exclaimed angrily. "Now he will be telling everyone that I am in the hands of the priests."

The room in which Rose was lying was always kept for Sir George when he visited Venice. It had, he used to say, the most beautiful view in the world and it would not have been easy to prove him wrong. He opened the door without knocking and looked in quietly, and a very dark young nun with a moustache and a bad squint sprang to her feet. Rose was lying, propped up in bed with her fleece of dark hair tangled in witch's stirrups and hanging over her flushed cheeks. Her eyes sparkled. Her right arm lay in a splint across the turned-down sheet.

"Oh, darling, I've been waiting for you with such impatience!"

Sir George nodded familiarly to the nun and embraced Rose long and tenderly; then he perched himself on the bed and began to stroke her hair. The nun subsided and began to read her book.

"I had begun to think you had gone straight to that Giulietta creature and was preparing to follow you to her villa."

"What's all this stuff about your dying in delirium?" asked Sir George, kissing her again.

"It's not my fault really. It's yours for running away. And of course that wretched Alexis. Oh, I got so angry with him! I haven't been so angry with anyone for years. And then the fool pretended to know all about wounds and knew nothing. He said it was a mere flesh wound, so I set off here next morning, without showing it to anyone—but he was wrong and I ran a high fever."

"You seem to have upset Leonardo a good deal."

"Do the horrible creature good."

"He says you were very indiscreet talking about Alexis trying to murder you and my running away to take refuge with Giulietta."

"Well, I'm a bit vague. Anyway Alexis was wrong about this damned arm. It has been torture. I was raving when I got here. There must have been some horrible bugs in Elizabeth's pillow-case. I've been at the mercy of a doctor who smells of stale fish and this infernal young woman gives me the creeps with that squint of hers. You must take charge now. You can give me the bedpan just as well as she can. With your nursing I shall soon get well. Chase her out. Or are you going to desert me on my deathbed?"

And Rose suddenly gave a full-blooded laugh at her own words.

"My dramatic talent takes control when my temperature rises above thirty-nine degrees." She went on laughing, half hysterically, while Sir George stroked her hair and said nothing. Half an hour later the nun closed her book, packed her bag and departed and Sir George took over her functions.

"She had a very nasty infection with the first signs of a generalised septicaemia, but she's all right now," said the discreet doctor, who did smell of stale fish, for the good reason that he was a passionate sea angler and kept sand eels in his pockets. "Penicillin and the constitution of an ox will work miracles. But the motor nerve is cut and she will not be able to lift her arm until it chooses to grow again—it takes about six months usually, but it may be less as she has such a strong will. Make her keep on trying to lift it."

"I can have a real holiday now, thanks to Alexis," said Rose after he had gone away. "There is no possibility of my acting Lady Macbeth with a paralysed arm, is there?"

Three days later Rose was well enough to go out with her arm in a sling and drink iced coffee at Florian's, and after that her progress was rapid. She had never been to Venice before. For six weeks they lived in that extraordinary town, getting up early, sleeping and making love in the afternoons and dining late, at some little restaurant—the *Città di Milano* was their favourite—eating lobsters or *scampi* and stuffed aubergines and finishing their meal with enormous *zabaglione*, whipped so stiff that the spoon would stand upright in the brownish yellow froth of egg-yolk and marsala. Sometimes they chose dishes that Rose could eat with one hand, sometimes the head waiter cut up her meat for her, making it into an act of intimacy and homage to her beauty.

Then, after the last little cups of black *espresso* coffee and the last sips of brandy, they would stroll side by side through the little streets, losing themselves in the alleys between the Accademia and the Rialto bridge, pausing on romantic bridges beside which barges piled high with water-melons were tied up.

In the mornings they would visit palaces and museums and Sir George would stand for ten minutes in front of *La Vecchia* by Giorgione.

"The most revolutionary painting that I know of —pointing the way to Rembrandt and the moderns —the work of the first artist whose eyes were opened to the beauty of old age."

Rose laughed at his enthusiasm and asked where he had read it and was surprised when he said shyly that probably what he had said was a commonplace but that he could not remember reading about the picture.

When she heard that Sir George and Rose were staying in Venice, the Marchesa Trapani invited them to stay for a weekend at her villa. Sir George took his car out of the great six-storey garage and they drove north into the hills. Giulietta was an artist, she was young, beautiful, extremely well-educated and intelligent. She talked eagerly, sometimes touching the person she was addressing as only children do in England, and her words were punctuated by intimate glances and inexplicably delightful little laughs. She talked French fluently but rather badly, and perfect English, but during their visit they kept to the former language for Rose's sake.

Giulietta was small and slim and brown with black hair falling on to her shoulders, an aquiline nose and black eyes gleaming through beautifully cut narrow eyelids. Sir George introduced Rose and went back to the car, leaving the two women together. In five minutes Rose had forgotten her jealousy and had fallen in love with the Italian woman.

All except four rooms of her sixteenth-century villa were shut up as she was very poor, but she earned a little money by contributing to an American encyclopaedia. The first night they sat up talking till two o'clock in the morning, drinking some of the China tea which Sir George had brought Giulietta as a present, Giulietta drawing Rose out eagerly about her early experiences as an actress. Finally, George said he was sleepy and Rose and he went to their bedroom and Rose said:

"But she is wonderful; she is the first woman who has ever made me feel clumsy and coarse. How can you love me? Why are you not in love with her?"

Sir George shrugged his shoulders, gave her a long look out of his innocent blue eyes and kissed her. He had been on the point of saying: "But Giulietta has a lover," which would have been disastrous.

Next morning he closeted himself in a little summer house with pen and paper and said he did not want to be disturbed, and the two women spent the morning making beds and cooking. When they had eaten lunch Sir George refused to accompany them bathing and went on with his poem until he fell asleep. That evening Rose's words were: "I am in love with your Giulietta and I think she returns my feelings a little," and this time Sir George did not hesitate to say: "But Giulietta has a lover."

"Yes," Rose said regretfully. "She told me about him and she spoke about you also."

"What did she say about me?"

"She told me that she felt a tremendous physical attraction for you. And I don't mind at all. Green-eyed people are not always jealous, are they?"

"Giulietta thinks I am a good poet, you know. But I don't suppose she's right."

However, next day he read aloud his poem to Giulietta while Rose lay on a sofa watching them out of her green cat's eyes. After ten minutes both reader and listener noticed that she was asleep. And when the poem was finished Sir George told Giulietta the whole story of Rose and Alexis in Pau and in Paris.

On their return to Venice they dined with an English friend of Sir George's in his palace, and Rose was again enchanted, though without the physical intimacy she had felt for Giulietta. However, she rather fell in love with his moustache. One of her wishes, that Sir George had steadily ignored, was that he should grow one. They went together on excursions to Chioggia, to Torcello and to Murano. They bathed occasionally at the Lido and would have done so more often if Rose had not felt handicapped in swimming by her paralysed arm. They were happy, yet as the summer went on Rose became restless. The mosquitoes by night and the swarms of German trippers by day became intolerable. And the spectacle of the young Venetian men following the flaxen-haired Gretchens, in their *dirndls* and their shorts about the streets, whistling at them or pinching their bottoms, disgusted her far more than it did Sir George.

"Since they have inherited the most beautiful city in the world, they should learn how to behave themselves," she said severely.

Tiring of Venice they packed their belongings, loaded the car and set off to the lakes and the mountains and then descended to the plains.

One afternoon in October they were sitting in the little square of Bergamo Old Town drinking coffee, when Rose said:

"Will you promise to agree to what I am going to ask you?"

"I may as well. You will get your own way anyhow."

"Will you promise not to laugh at me?"

"You are going to tell me that you think you can play Lady Macbeth quite well with a bloody spot on your paralysed hand and that not being able to move it is a wonderful dramatic invention which will delight the critics."

Rose looked daggers at him and roared with laughter.

"Quite the contrary. But don't tease me or laugh at me or you will make me unhappy."

"I never tease you or make you unhappy laughing at you. But come on, out with it."

"I want you to marry me."

Sir George beckoned to the waiter who was hovering near them.

"Two more *espressos*, please." He waited until the man had gone and then said: "What's the idea?"

Rose touched her arm. "This would never have happened if we had been married."

"Locking the stable door after the horse is stolen, as we say in England."

"What do you mean, darling?"

"Well, you don't think Alexis will come back and shoot you again, do you? There's no one else hanging around with a pistol, is there?"

"That wasn't the real reason. I want to have a baby."

"Oh, my dear creature. You'll be desperately anxious to be back on the stage long before nine months are up. You can move your arm a little already. Isn't it just a sudden idea, because you feel you are wasting your time?"

The waiter had come back with the coffee. Sir George paid him, but the man stood watching them intently. He knew French. Rose shook her head.

"I've been wanting to speak for the last month. I talked about it to Giulietta."

"Did you now? Well, I can't guarantee success— but I'll do my best. Fetch me a bottle of ink." The last words were addressed to the waiter.

"Will you marry me anyhow?"

"Whenever you like. Didn't I promise to do whatever you asked?"

Rose took hold of his thin brown hand, uncurled the long fingers and kissed the palm.

Sir George and Rose were married a few weeks later in front of the English Consul in Genoa and Giulietta came across Italy to be a witness and to offer to lend them her villa for their honeymoon. She brought her lover with her: a pale young poet who smiled politely the whole time that he was there. Sir George kissed Giulietta until she said: "But I am not the bride. I am the best man and I claim the best man's privileges," and she embraced Rose so passionately that Signor Bruno went and looked out of the window. Sir George was delighted by this.

His first efforts at parenthood seemed to have been successful and Rose would exclaim excitedly after breakfast:

"I feel a slight sensation of nausea. It must be the real thing. Isn't it wonderful?"

"Don't get excited. We have plenty of time."

"I may want to have six children."

"You should have thought of that earlier."

"If it's a boy I'm going to call him Bergamo."

"Bergamot. Sir Bergamot Dillingham. I say, if it's a boy the baronetcy will not become extinct. I never thought of that."

"You should have thought of that earlier."

Thereafter they spoke of Bergamot when they talked of the child to be born.

The marriage had been announced in *The Times* and brought, among other letters, one from Alexis to Rose who opened it and read it aloud.

Dear Rose,

I congratulate you on getting what you wanted and hope you will be happy. You seem to have given up the stage, I hope not permanently. I have gone back into the army—for keeps. I am being posted to Germany and may occasionally be sent to Paris. But it is a large town. If only your marriage had occurred before my return from Malaya, I should not have to reproach myself with an act of criminal folly. Congratulations to Uncle George.

Yours ever, Alexis

"A rotten letter. The brute insinuates that it was your immoral conduct which led him to try and murder me," said Rose. Sir George said nothing. Later that day, when they were sitting over the dinner table, she returned to the subject.

"That God-damn letter has left a God-damn bad taste in my mouth."

Rose had been reading the history of Jeanne d'Arc and the French nickname for the English soldiers—*les god-damns*—was temporarily being applied to everything.

"A God-damn letter. Don't you agree?"

"Well, it was nice of him to write, but it was difficult for him to strike a happy mean and his feelings come out more than he intended, I think," said George.

"Don't let's talk of him. That boy was born to make us quarrel."

"We owe a great deal to him."

"Such as?" said Rose in the light tone of voice

which always preceded her losing her temper and which she had scarcely ever used to Sir George.

"Meeting each other in the first place; marrying in the second; starting a child in the third."

Rose could not deny his words and ruminated sullenly.

The nerve in Rose's arm was growing together as predicted and she was able by an intense effort of will to raise her elbow a few centimetres. In order to encourage her, Sir George invented an ingenious form of torture and persuaded her to accept it. She was only allowed a glass of wine, or an aperitif, if she could lift it to her mouth with her right hand. It was easy enough for her to lift it, but tipping the glass to the horizontal was more than she could manage. Now Rose tried to calm her ruffled feelings by taking a drink and struggled for a little while vainly to get more than a sip.

Suddenly she burst into her warm, good-tempered laugh.

"You God-damn Englishman. You owe him more than I do. Getting away with all the drinks."

"Darling, you shall have one on the house for that remark."

And Sir George filled his own glass and held it to her lips.

When she had finished drinking it, she reverted to the subject, but in a very different tone.

"You are always trying to make excuses for him," she said at last. "I believe you are still trying to bring him back into our lives, though you don't really like him as much as I do."

"On the contrary. I have come to the conclusion that we had better not see him again."

"I have no particular intention of ever seeing him again. But I should not refuse to do so if he turned up," said Rose.

"That would be a nasty thing to do. But if the opportunity arises and it is possible to avoid it, let us do so. He's a bit unbalanced," said Sir George.

"You think he's mad because he was desperately in love with me," said Rose crossly, and a moment later gave a roar of laughter.

"Well, the form it took was a bit mad. I think you like him all the better for it. I suppose you were really rather flattered."

"It was more flattering than seizing the chance to run away from me. But you are not usually so stupid as to think that my vanity was satisfied by that horrible incident. Of course Alexis was intolerable. But it was a good deal because I was such an unimaginative bitch. I was thinking about you and Giulietta all the time, and never told him. Anyway I've forgiven him. That's why his letter seems so rotten."

"I'm glad you have forgiven him. For some reason I haven't. I have a feeling that he took advantage of a moment of altruism in me."

"I don't quite accept that," said Rose. "What you mean is that owing to some guilty feelings you have about me, you bear him a grudge because he imposed on you when you were ready to give me up. But wasn't the real reason for what you call altruism that you had Giulietta up your sleeve, all the time?"

Sir George said nothing. A moment later he got up and left the room. Rose could see that she had wounded him.

Ten minutes later she followed him.

"It was vulgar and ungenerous of me to say that. Please forgive me."

Sir George kissed her and said nothing.

"I want to grow wine in my old age," he remarked next morning.

"Let us go to France," said Rose.

"I cannot face the *mistral* or I would choose Provence. The best wine is grown in Médoc which, except for the Sauternes district, is rather ugly—and a long way from Paris. Moreover, I don't like sweet white wine like Sauternes. I don't care for the landscape of Burgundy—where shall it be?" asked Sir George.

"Anjou or Touraine, where I come from. You remember that I come from near Chinon," said Rose.

"I had forgotten. Come here, Gargamelle. Our son will have to be called Gargantua. We shall have to provide wine enough for such a child as he will be."

Rose wrote to her uncle, a solicitor in Chinon, and some weeks later received a letter saying that he could recommend a small property for sale, but that the price was high. There were, however, various attractions. It was situated on the crest of the hill within a stone's throw of Rabelais' birthplace, *La Devinière*, and overlooking it. The small farmhouse and the barns and *chai* were remains of ancient monastic buildings which had been part of the Abbey of Seuilly. Most important was that the vineyard of about fifteen acres was planted with ancient vines which produced a most excellent red wine of eleven or twelve per cent alcoholic strength, for which there was a ready sale.

"Actually this is the wine which Rabelais first tasted, a fact which may appeal to your husband who has, I think, literary interests."

Directly after receiving this letter they drove to Chinon, garaged the Rolls, put on their oldest clothes and drove out next day in a hired car, for the appearance of wealth had to be avoided.

Chinon itself and the flat stretches of the Loire country had depressed Sir George, but directly the car turned off the main road and began to crawl up the lane which led to Seuilly, his spirits rose. Once they reached the top of the hill and saw the view, his mind was made up. To the north they could look across the river Vienne to the plateau of Bourgeuil; to the East the whole of the battlefield in the war against Picrochole, described by Rabelais, lay at their feet. As he stood and gazed, Sir George became aware of a quality in the landscape which he could only describe as goodness. It was early May: the young shoots were sprouting from the old stumps of the vines; the earth was covered with spring flowers; the first roses were in blossom on the old fourteenth-century stone walls. Everything welcomed him with the smiling promise of simplicity and peace. No evil could come to such a place. He would end his days close to where Rabelais was born.

Once he had made up his mind he threw himself into practical details while Rose rested in the cool tiled kitchen. Then, when he had walked round the vineyard and the paddocks, had inspected the wine-press and the long dark *chai*, built more than half underground, he came back and signed the agreement which Rose's uncle had drawn up. The bargain was sealed with glasses of the oldest wine in the cellar. Then he went back to the *chai* with the widow who was selling the property, to taste the wine of the previous year.

"Don't drink it too young," she said.

"If I don't drink it when I can, I may not drink it at all," he said. She was delighted.

George took all the practical affairs of settling in to the farm on his shoulders. To buy it he had to sell not only *Les Pervenches* but the lease of his flat in Paris and two of his best pictures. He furnished the house from the villa at Pau and he engaged a girl called Gabrielle as a servant and nurse.

When the time for Rose's confinement approached, she suggested trying to bribe their neighbour, the delightful peasant woman who took the tourists round the room in which Rabelais was born, to allow Bergamot to be born in it. What would have been impossible in Stratford-on-Avon might with much laughter and luck have been achieved at Chinon. But Sir George was far too anxious about her to encourage the idea. Rose was safely delivered of a daughter by the village midwife in their little farmhouse where the amenities chiefly differed from those of the fifteenth century in the presence of a wad of cotton wool soaked in chloroform and ether, and in an abundance of dettol and hot water.

The sex of the child was a disappointment: Bergamot would never be a baronet. The child was named Jeanne and almost immediately called Jenny. She was strong and sturdy, with her father's delicate complexion and her mother's dark tawny hair. When her eyes lost the opacity of a new-born baby's, they were seen to be neither green nor pure blue, but grey. Rose's confinement had been easy and after three days she refused to remain any longer in bed.

A week after the birth of Jenny had been announced in *The Times*, a letter arrived for Rose in Alexis's handwriting. George took it out on to the terrace to where she was suckling Jenny.

"You read it to me, darling."

Sir George slit the envelope, took out the letter and read:

Dear Rose,

My very warmest congratulations. The news filled me with joy, not only because it so abundantly justifies your marriage, but because it explains your absence from the stage and will, I hope, herald your return to it in some months' time.

I deeply regret my folly and wickedness. Each of us belongs to himself and not to another. My intense passion for you blinded me to this and my life appeared unendurable unless I could bind you to my delight. If time should soften your resentment and contempt, it would make me very happy to be allowed to see my little cousin. I hope she will inherit her mother's beauty, strength and talent and her father's goodness and poetical gift. Please give him my love.

Yours ever, Alexis

"Well, that is a charming and delightful letter. I'll write back at once and ask him to come and see Jenny when we get back to Paris."

Sir George said nothing and Rose looked up from her baby at him. When he met her eye, he asked: "Must you?"

"You don't like his letter then?"

"No, I do like it. He has been reading Blake and it is nice of him to write: but it does not follow that he has changed."

"It is you who have changed, George. You used always to be standing up for him. I shall never forget your saying that it was your fault, not his when he tried to murder me. I shall never forget that."

"We have been through all this a dozen times. Perhaps I have changed. But I don't like emotional postmortems. I am happy in my old age. Alexis has done enough mischief."

"He won't do any more. And I want to show him Jenny."

"If it doesn't come out in one way, it will in another."

Rose, however, wrote back a friendly letter and asked Alexis to invite himself to *La Grange* for a night if he had the opportunity.

Shortly after this something occurred which interfered with her plans of going back to act in Marcel's company in the autumn. One morning the postman brought Sir George a long envelope with an English stamp. He read it and remained sitting for some time motionless, looking out of the window. In front of him, close at hand, were the serried ranks of the vines, their dark foliage lightly coated with a blue veneer of copper sulphate. It was, or so Sir George liked to maintain, the very vineyard from which Brother John drove the followers of Picrochole when they were pillaging the grapes, by laying about him with the staff of the cross.

Beyond it were the strips of arable fields: the dark green stripe of lucerne standing against the yellow of barley stubble, the pale green of dried-up pasture, grey willows, and beyond, on the opposite slope, the castle in which Picrochole had taken up his quarters.

After a time he got up and, taking the letter, went to find Rose. She was asleep under the mulberry tree, with Jenny asleep in her basket-work cradle close by.

Rose's big breasts, swollen with milk, had burst a button on her bodice and were half uncovered; her tawny hair had come down in an untidy mass in which a dead twig or two had been caught up. The corners of her full mouth were stained with mulberry juice. The brown sunburn of her neck faded gradually into the golden ivory of her shoulder and breast. One of her bare brown legs was uncovered from the knee. Sir George looked at her. She had never been more splendid. Presently he lay down on the grass beside her and, leaning on his elbow, waited, watching her.

After a few minutes she moved, opened her big green eyes, shook her head sleepily, and said:

"I didn't know you were there. What is it?"

"Are you properly awake?"

Rose nodded.

"I have lost most of my money. We are practically ruined. You remember that old friend whom I financed?"

"That man who came to lunch on the island and called me: 'Rose darling,' the first time he met me—the big man with ugly ears?"

"He writes that the capital is lost. I must either agree to my shares being written down, or put it in the hands of the Official Receiver. Either way my money is lost."

Rose stuck out her lower lip and brooded. There was a sound beside her and she saw that George's eyes were screwed up and that there were tears in the wrinkles of his cheeks. Rose sat up, put her arms round his shoulders and pulled him towards her. As she kissed him he began to sob.

"I am an old fool and shall always be one. He knew perfectly well that his shares were worth nothing when he got the last ten thousand out of me. The letters he wrote: about my poems, the view from my room, the warm messages to you. I thought I knew him quite well and all the time every word of this friend and business associate was calculated. Every word was inspired by an ulterior motive."

"Darling, the money doesn't matter."

"Oh, yes it does. I have you and Jenny to think about."

"I'll do a film. That Italian is always writing. He wrote only six weeks ago and it seemed so funny because I was the size of a barrel."

They did not go back to Paris in the autumn. Rose spent three months in Sardinia acting in a film about starving fishermen and George remained working at *La Grange* and looking after Jenny. The vintage was over when Rose returned for a few weeks' rest before appearing in a play that Marcel was putting on in Paris for the Christmas season. When she went, George again remained with Gabrielle and Jenny and, except that he went up for the first three nights of the play, did not see Rose for another two months. She achieved a triumph on the stage and the picture was an immense success. In the winter she took a month's holiday before starting on another picture.

This separated existence became the pattern of their lives. Rose would be away for three or four months at a stretch and then would return exhausted, rich and triumphant, to the farm.

The new wine would be compared with the old; the calf born in her absence would be admired, and she would discuss the details of her career; Marcel wanted her for a play by Goldoni, but there was a chance of her acting in a new film by Cocteau—which would be more lucrative and amusing.

At intervals George, accompanied by Jenny and Gabrielle, would visit Paris for a week or two. His silver hair, wild rose complexion and blue eyes were usually to be seen at the first nights of the plays and the premières of the films in which Rose appeared, and on these occasions George was a dignified and aristocratic figure in perfectly cut clothes.

But during the *entractes* his thoughts wandered: would it be worth going to the *marché aux puces* to look for a real old-fashioned rocking-horse for Jenny? And he must go to Vilmorin's to get a new valve for the spraying machine for the vines.

Rose became a well-to-do woman. She invested her money imprudently in Government securities, but she spent it also on things she liked. She bought herself a huge new Rolls-Royce car in which she drove herself everywhere and she took the ground floor of a very ancient house on the left bank of the river in the Rue Christine. At first, when she was in Paris, she lived there with an older woman, a scene designer. Their big studio was usually full of young men, all of them infatuated with Rose. Sometimes she would be very nice to one or other of them for a week or two, then she would abruptly dismiss him, telling him angrily that her life was perfect and that she detested complications.

Part Four

Ten years after the birth of Jenny, Alexis arrived in Paris, where he was to take up a fairly important inter-allied military post. He was thirty and a Lieutenant-Colonel, but the army bored him and often he asked himself why he should go on. Was it merely because he was extremely successful? He had begun to write a story: but success as a writer seemed impossible.

The morning after his arrival he picked up a copy of *La Semaine de Paris* and saw that that evening was the last night of Turgenev's *A Month in the Country*, in which Rose would be playing Natalya Petrovna opposite Vilars as Rakitin. If Rose had developed as he hoped, it would be a wonderful combination. His new secretary was able to get him a seat in the stalls and, after a little hesitation, he sent Rose the following note by the *pneumatique*:

> "I have just arrived in Paris and shall see your performance tonight. May I come round afterwards to your dressing-room for a moment?—Alexis."

It was a lovely summer's day. Paris had never looked more beautiful, and half an hour after he had sent off his *petit bleu*, he was invited by his opposite number, a French officer who would be working with him in the same room, to have lunch with him at *Le Bleu* restaurant. It would have been a pleasant beginning to their relationship, but Alexis said he had a prior engagement and refused. It would be ridiculous to wait in his hotel the whole day in the hope that Rose would reply. Everything had come to an end between them eleven years before. He did not want to renew relations with her, even if it were possible to do so. Yet he knew that he would wait in the whole of the afternoon and that if she did not answer, his unhappiness would be out of all proportion to his rational feeling for her. Why, he asked himself, should he have this agony of uncertainty, this thrill of insane expectation?

Alexis had enjoyed love affairs with women and friendships with them, since he had last seen Rose, but he had not felt for a single one of them the agitation which kept him in his room.

"A telephone call for you, sir. Will you take it?"

"Certainly."

"Alexis! How wonderful! Are you free? Are you alone? Come round to my studio this minute. I have got some people to lunch, but you will stay. Oh! I am so delighted to be going to see you at last."

The studio was through an old archway in the Rue Christine.

There was a courtyard, an open doorway which led into a dirty hall with a wide eighteenth-century staircase into which a ramshackle little lift had been inserted. Alexis was in a state of emotional agitation: he was doing at last what six years before he had often been tempted to do but which, when the opportunity had offered, he had always resisted. Now after six years in Africa, he had written to Rose at the first possible moment. And all his conscious thoughts were filled with her. But war in the jungle had sharpened his unconscious intuitions. The entrance to the studio struck him as evil. Alexis had become extremely sensitive to danger. There was, he felt, a lurking hostility in the hall. He was going into danger. This sensation was so absolutely unexpected that he looked about him in a puzzled way after he had rung the bell.

The next moment Rose was standing in the doorway. She had grown fatter: she was also taller and far more beautiful than he remembered.

"I'm just back from six years in Africa," he said.

She put her arms round him and kissed him warmly.

"Straight from the jungle. Just like last time. Well, I'm not afraid."

"I am. I felt that this place was dangerous," said Alexis.

Rose stared at him, puzzled. Then she led him into a big room, put her arms round him again and kissed him on both cheeks as though she wished to repeat in public what she had already done on the doorstep.

"My nephew, Colonel Golightly."

Alexis found himself being introduced to a woman of fifty, to a young girl called Vivienne, and to three young men, all of whom seemed to be ten years his junior.

The other people in the room shook hands but immediately reverted to the subject which they had been discussing, on which the elderly lady was laying down the law. Slowly Alexis made out that Vivienne's girl friend had insisted on playing records of a music hall singer for whom she had conceived a passion. Vivienne had asked her to stop, but no attention had been paid to her request. Finally, when the other girl's back was turned, Vivienne had thrown the records out of the window. Her friend had not spoken to her since. The subjects under debate were: What was going to happen tomorrow? What were the psychological causes of her action? Was it jealousy or was it boredom?

The details of this storm in a teacup were discussed at enormous length, and Rose was continually called in to give an opinion. Vivienne even asked Alexis to give an impartial judgment. The chatter of these people exasperated him and he found it difficult not to show either boredom or impatience.

At last they sat down to lunch. Rose kept him beside her, asked him about Africa and told him about a film she had made in Algeria. To see Rose in such surroundings was maddening and revealing—yet, what more had he expected?

Finally, when irritation had got the better of him and he rose to go, she said: "Come and talk to me for a few minutes alone."

Alexis followed her into a room which was half bedroom and half office, for it contained filing cabinets and a dictaphone as well as a luxuriously comfortable double bed.

"No, not that," she said when he put a hand on her shoulder. "I did not ask you in here to make love to me, but so that we could talk freely. You know that I am very fond of you, Alexis. I just wanted to tell you so. How long will you be in Paris? Are you free for the next few days? I should like to invite you to come down and see Jenny. You know George and I have established ourselves near Chinon. I am driving down there. Would you like to come with me?"

"Are you sure you want me to come?"

"Of course I'm sure. As soon as the performance is over I shall come back here, snatch two hours' sleep and then set off at four o'clock in the morning. We shall be there at eight o'clock—in time for breakfast."

In everything she said he was aware of the old intimacy and the complicity of shared secrets. As she went on talking, he felt forgotten emotions stirring in him. Already they were involved in a sweet conspiracy which was intoxicating and of which he did not even wish to divine the ending.

Rose was saying: "You must pack the things you want for a couple of days. Bring your bag to the theatre with you and put it in my car before the performance. I'll leave the key with the stage-doorkeeper and ask him to show you where it is parked."

Her words and her totally unexpected invitation produced such a reaction that Alexis was overcome. The face of the soldier, coarsened by life in the tropics, made wooden by years of formality, set and moulded by the futilities of staff work and the frustrations which any intelligent officer learns to accept as the very nature and condition of life, began to pucker into the unwonted creases of childhood and his lips trembled.

"You are so kind. How can you ever forgive me? You are so good."

"Don't be such a fool. What a silly child you are," said Rose. "I feel a very tender friendship for you. But don't let's talk about it now." She kissed him impulsively and went on with instructions.

"Don't come to my dressing-room afterwards, but let yourself into the car. If you sit in the back seat and don't turn the light on, nobody will notice you. It will save time."

Alexis went away wondering if he were on his head or his heels.

It was so long since he had been in a theatre, or had seen good acting, that when the lights went up for the first interval, he felt numb. "What strange art is this," he reflected, "that transposes reality? What we think of as the real world—that fat man with his bald head, that aging woman with her powdered wrinkles eyeing the audience like a hen uncertain whether to cross the road—they turn out to be so trivial and ephemeral as to have no existence, and then, when the lights go down, the curtain rises and we meet real people, real emotions, and are carried into eternity. With her perpetual reincarnations this Russian land-owner's wife, modelled on Turgenev's mistress, Pauline Viardot, has a reality that Pauline or Rose could never achieve in their lives."

That evening Alexis felt himself reborn: the tears were pricking his eyelids: he felt a concentration of all his forces. "I might have been a poet and play-wright; I might have written something which would have had the kind of eternal reality I find in Turgenev. I may have missed my chance but I have it in me. At all events I have a reality greater than the men around me."

He got up during the interval and went into the foyer to smoke a cigarette and, feeling for his matches, accidentally touched the key of Rose's car, which the doorkeeper had given him. The touch of the metal sent a shiver of gratified vanity and of self-confidence through him. It was going to be all right. There was the talisman to prove it. Holding the key in his pocket he looked about him at the crowd of unhealthy-looking men and observant ladies with contempt.

"They are shadows. I alone am alive because Rose, who is Natalya Petrovna, has given me this key and told me to hide in the back of her car."

At the conclusion of the play there were seven curtains.

Alexis went out and took his seat in Rose's car, asking himself whether, like Rakitin, he was destined to become Rose's *cavaliere servente*, while she fell in love with one young man after another. Fate might play that strange trick.

"Don't talk to me, darling," said Rose when she had driven out of the press of cars leaving the theatre. "I can't bear another word. Just a bowl of soup and a couple of hours' sleep and I shall be alive again." Alexis was silent.

In the studio they drank soup, and a few moments later, after pointing to a sofa, Rose went to her bed-room.

Alexis lay down to rest, but he did not sleep. The exaltation which had made everything appear unreal except the play with Rose its centre, an exaltation which had persisted when he silently followed her into the studio through the evil doorway and had obediently lapped up the soup set before him—that afflatus had ended. Lying on the sofa, he reverted from being a boy of twenty to being a man of thirty. He began an accountancy of his gains and losses during the day.

"I have discovered that Rose feels no hostility towards me because of the past. She cares for me, but the idea of taking me as a lover has not occurred to her as possible. I do not think she will ever feel for me in that way again. Yet she would not be taking me on this trip unless there was something which she wants from me and that apparently I alone may be able to supply. What is it? It is something to do with her life with George and Jenny. Something not to be found in Paris—therefore connected with them. I must be extremely careful not to betray any hope of becoming her lover. It must be for her to make the first approach, if any is made. Meanwhile it washes out my flying back to London for the weekend to see Janet. Paris and Touraine take the place of Campden Hill and Pulborough."

With that thought he closed his eyes and lay motionless and, though still conscious, it was with surprise that he heard Rose calling to him.

"Come and have a bath or a shower while I make the coffee, it will make you feel wonderful." She switched on the light and he looked up to see her standing near him. Her body was naked and wet under the big towel she had wrapped round it. Little trickles of water were running from her hair down her shoulders. Turning, she went back into the bathroom, leaving dark prints of her wet feet upon the parquet floor.

Rose had come to fetch him without the faintest coquetry. It seemed perfectly natural to her to call him to share her bath. The idea of his being her lover was at that moment completely absent from her mind and she was in a hurry to get on the road. Yet she would not have been so free with him if Alexis had not been her lover in the past. But she had no thought of him as a lover in the future.

It was perhaps as well that Alexis had been summing up his probable relations with her. For it needed all his self-control to follow her into the bathroom and begin undressing without looking at her in a special way while she rubbed her legs vigorously, put on her stockings and her skirt and pulled a black jersey over her silk chemise.

"Don't be more than a couple of minutes," she said, going into the kitchen, but leaving the door open so that she could go on talking.

The Paris streets were almost empty and on the road to Orleans there were only rare lorries. Although it was summer, Rose had slipped a fur coat over her black jersey. Once or twice as the car swung on a bend Alexis felt the fur touch his cheek and he caught a whiff of her perfume. He had taken out his cigar-case and was on the point of lighting a cheroot when the thought that smoking would kill the scent of Rose's presence made him put it back into his pocket.

"What did you think of last night's performance? Of course I must confess I'm a good deal like Natalya Petrovna, so it's an easy part for me. I only have to be myself. Vilars is magnificent; he is Rakitin to the life."

Alexis told her his feelings about the dreamlike character of the audience and the eternal reality of the play.

"I often feel like that about my own life when I am living in Paris and acting. But we are all real enough down at *La Grange*. Jenny is as real as Vera." Rose laughed a little.

"She is purely intellectual so far. George is madly in love with her. I am the third party in our *ménage*. If you fall in love with her, as you inevitably will, I shall be delighted. But George may become jealous, which would be amusing."

"Does he know I'm coming?" asked Alexis, suddenly anxious.

"I sent him a telegram."

They had been driving through forests for a long way. Suddenly the road emerged into open undulating country. Rose-pink clouds dotted the sky and an immense flush of fire and gold spread rapidly. Already a few peasants were coming to work in the fields. An old man by the roadside was sharpening a scythe, a young woman with a bucket was walking towards a tethered cow.

"How old is Jenny?"

"Ten."

Alexis smiled. It seemed improbable that Rose should have invited him to stay at *La Grange* so that he should fall in love with a child of ten and it was amusing that he should have sacrificed Janet for one. Would she be more or less exasperated if she knew that she had been thrown over for a child? The fact appeared to be that Rose wanted to share Jenny with him: George was perhaps too possessive.

With that thought, his whole state of mind changed: his earlier exaltation had been followed by speculation and analysis, in which he had tried to achieve detachment. But he suddenly felt that he had missed the point. Rose was warm; was bursting with affection. Her character had expanded and been enriched by success. She wanted to share her emotions with an old friend.

He was completely at ease and good-tempered and he gave Rose a nudge.

"Hein? What's biting you?"

"Only you've turned out to be such an awfully nice woman."

Rose laughed. "Oh, these Englishmen! What rewards I get for my devotion. 'An awfully nice woman.' I'll get George to put it on my tombstone if, as seems likely, he survives me."

She put the car out of gear and after coasting for some way, brought it to a standstill beside where some apple trees bordered the road.

"Coffee?"

Alexis drank and stared contentedly at Rose; she noticed it at last and she smiled questioningly.

"Where are you taking me?" he asked for the sake of saying something.

She started the car. "George has a passion for Rabelais which always seems to me rather peculiar in him. Because he is really very refined in his habits. It's one of the things which makes him so agreeable to live with. Anyhow, we live very close to where Rabelais may have been born and where he certainly lived as a child. No doubt he drank the wine from our vineyard and our view is the same as the one from his attic. All that means an immense amount to George."

"Is that why you went there?"

"No. It happens to be my country. My family have lived near Chinon for generations. George says, and it is the best compliment he has ever paid me, that I am just like our wine: strong but not very subtle: beautiful, even delicious, but always leaving one with a clear head."

"George must have a stronger head than I have. I find you quite intoxicating," said Alexis.

"Not at half-past six in the morning. But you wait till you meet Jenny. She is more subtle than I am. It is her English blood, no doubt."

Alexis laughed, but he knew that Rose was perfectly serious; there was no trace of irony in her words and as he agreed with her about English subtlety he said nothing.

George and Jenny had waited for their arrival to have breakfast. Alexis had only the time to see that his uncle was stouter, that he held himself upright but that the delicate skin had been invaded by a close network of lines and wrinkles, that the hair which had been thick and grey was silver and growing thin, and then that Jenny was tall, had very full lips and that, after her first rapturous welcome, she became very calm. Then Gabrielle brought in the *espresso* coffee machine and a large saucepan of hot milk and they sat down to a breakfast of hot rolls, home-made butter with half-melting brown honey and bitter marmalade. Jenny asked him if he would like eggs and bacon, but he refused. There was obvious mockery in the offer, as well as politeness.

The room was immense: It had been an outlying barn belonging to the Abbey of Seuilly, but George had converted it into the kitchen and dining-room: they slept in the small farmhouse the other side of the courtyard.

Five hours later Sir George was taking his usual siesta, but he was not asleep, only dozing, when he heard Alexis and Jenny sit down on the stone seat directly outside his study. They were talking English and on this occasion Sir George did not scruple to eavesdrop.

Jenny was saying: "Well, if you believe in mermaids I might be one, for all you know. What would you do then?"

"You mean if you had a lovely silver tail instead of horrid knobbly knees, ugly calves and thick ankles?"

"Yes, a tail like a very big salmon," said Jenny, not in the least offended by the unflattering description of her legs.

"I should buy you one of those little motor bath-chair things. And you would earn lots of money performing in a circus in a tank with sea-lions."

"I wouldn't perform in a circus. The water in the tank would be dirty and the people would throw their cigarette ends into it."

"Well, if you won't perform in a circus you can always teach swimming in a fashionable girls' school."

"I should like that much better."

"Of course you would act in films. I think you could go on all your life acting in one film after another. There would be no competition. No other mermaid stars. You would be so popular that all the scripts would have a mermaid in them."

"With me singing and sitting on a rock and luring the sailors to destruction like in the *Odyssey*?"

"Those were sirens really and they had wings.

As a matter of fact mermaids are dumb and can't sing."

"You know nothing whatever about mermaids," exclaimed Jenny furiously. "Of course they sing. Why, mermaids are always singing as they comb their hair. That's what attracts the sailors."

"You know nothing about sailors."

That evening Sir George went out of his way to be particularly agreeable to Alexis. He opened two bottles of his best vintage wine and then made him try and compare two kinds of *marc* made from their own grapes. "Neither of them as old as they should be."

Finally, he invited him to come down for the vintage, an invitation which was enthusiastically repeated by Jenny.

For three years after that first visit Alexis became a frequent visitor to *La Grange*. He found there what he had never known since he was a small child—a home where he was welcome and where he felt that he belonged. He made himself very useful to Sir George by working hard on each of his visits and he found manual labour a delightful change after continual office work and endless committee meetings. He rebuilt, from a pile of tumbled-in masonry, a room like the transept of a church, which had at some distant time formed part of the barn in which they lived and had their meals. For two years he was able to take several days' leave at the time of the vintage and during it he worked from morning to night as a labourer in the fields. Sir George paid him his wages in wine, which kept him supplied in Paris.

Sometimes Rose was there during his visits, sometimes she was not. His real attachment was to the place and to Jenny.

As his feelings for the child grew, those for her mother became modified. Rose was no longer perfect, for he looked on her as the most powerful influence on Jenny's development and was by no means always sure that the influence was a good one. Sometimes also he was made angry by the degree to which Rose was unconscious of Jenny's feelings.

Though he was living and working in Paris and had a lot of free time, he did not often visit the studio in the Rue Christine. This was not because he had formed any attachments which he wished to keep apart from George, Rose and Jenny. He mixed a good deal with his fellow-officers, seeing as many American and British as he did French and Belgian; he was indeed extremely social, partly because he had no entanglements. But though he went several times to see any play or film in which Rose appeared, he avoided the studio. This was partly because of his changed feelings for Rose, partly because he had become aware that she had taken a boy of twenty called Vincent as her lover. Alexis had met him with Rose twice, and though he seemed a pleasant young fellow, his existence displeased him and he was annoyed with himself for this emotion.

The first occasion when the liaison was openly referred to was when he was staying for a few days at *La Grange*. Rose had arrived the night before and was due to stay a week. It was a lovely mild winter's morning and he was working alone, happily chipping the limestone sill for a window, when Rose suddenly appeared and said:

"I have got to go to Paris."

"What's the matter?"

"Vincent is ill and I must look after him. I thought perhaps you would not mind explaining it to Jenny when you fetch her from school."

"She'll be terribly disappointed. Isn't there anyone else who can look after the young man?"

Rose looked at him with surprise and said in the casual, conversational tone which he had learned to know so well, but had not heard her employ for many years: "I supposed you knew that he is living with me at the studio?"

Alexis must have betrayed some emotion, for she added:

"Surely you know that Vincent is my lover? The whole of Paris knows that." Alexis said nothing and she continued on a friendlier note:

"I am what other women call a baby-snatcher. I suppose it was you that started me off in that line and now I have reverted to it, so you need not look so confoundedly serious."

Alexis gave a laugh that rang a little false.

Rose's voice instantly became casual and she asked:

"Are you jealous by any chance, or what's the matter with you?"

"No, I'm not a bit jealous. But what am I to say to Jenny?"

"She knows Vincent. Tell her I have got to go to look after him, because he's ill. But make it sound natural."

"What about George?"

"Oh, I've told him I am going. There is no difficulty there."

"Good."

"Only as you will fetch her from school, I wanted you to tell Jenny at once."

Five minutes later Alexis saw the top of her Rolls sliding down the sunken lane which it almost completely filled.

Jenny's schooling was a subject on which Alexis secretly felt indignant. On his first visit to *La Grange* Jenny was attending the nearest village school like all the other children of the neighbourhood. Now, at thirteen, she was going to school in Chinon, to which Rose had expected her to bicycle every day. Alexis had, however, persuaded Sir George, without difficulty, that this was too much for her and now her father drove her to school in the mornings, leaving her to come home by bus. When Alexis visited *La Grange* he drove in after school and brought her home. Secretly he believed that she should go to school in Paris. That would mean, he realised, an entire transformation of her parents' lives. Alexis had taken it for granted that the uprooting of Sir George, who would not want to live alone at *La Grange*, was the only serious obstacle to be overcome. Now he saw that the presence of Vincent, as a permanent inmate of the studio, might be an even more important obstacle to his plan. He had intended to tackle Sir George and Rose together on this visit. This plan was inevitably postponed. It was lucky that he knew about Vincent. For though there was nothing actually impossible about his uncle and Vincent both living in the studio, it was out of the question for Jenny to do so also, since there were only two bedrooms.

The situation and the tactics to be employed in speaking to his uncle and to Rose filled his mind when he went to meet Jenny that afternoon. She was not waiting for him and eventually he went into the school buildings to find her. Although work was supposed to be over a quarter of an hour before, some of the classrooms were still crowded with children pressing round a teacher. The corridors were filled with wild little creatures dashing about, completely out of control, some yelling and some even attacking each other. The noise, untidiness, grubbiness and complete absence of any attempt at discipline revolted his military mind.

"My God, I'd bring them to heel or perish in the attempt," he thought. Though sympathetic when dealing with one child, Alexis was completely unimaginative when faced with a crowd of children. He saw them as recruits.

Jenny was found for him at last. She had lost all sense of time and was busy writing in a corner of an empty classroom.

"I'm writing something for *Maman*. It is a great secret. Promise not to breathe a word. It's a play for her to act in and there are parts for you and Vincent."

"Rose sent you a message. She has had to dash up to Paris suddenly because Vincent is ill and there is nobody to look after him."

Jenny nodded her head.

"Did *Maman* tell you what it was?"

"No, she didn't."

"I expect it's something pretty bad. Probably a haemorrhage. Vincent would never send for *Maman* unless he was really bad." And after paying Vincent this unexpected tribute, Jenny very deliberately changed the subject. It was clear that she was aware of the essentials of the situation.

Before Alexis left he spoke to his uncle in a purposely vague way about the desirability of Jenny's going to a really good school in Paris.

Sir George was most forthcoming. "I've given a lot of thought to it. I was even ready to send her off for a year to a school in England. Somewhere like Bedales. Rose would not hear of it. She maintains that the school in Chinon is excellent. It certainly has one very remarkable teacher on the staff. But I agree she really ought to go to Paris. I don't think it necessary immediately. But we must not put it off too long."

After his return to Paris Alexis went to see Rose.

"How is Vincent?" he asked as there was no sign of that young man in the studio.

"He has got t.b. Didn't you know? He had a bad haemorrhage and I found him in a frightful state. I simply had to put him in an aeroplane and fly with him to Switzerland. And he's at Montana for the next three months at least."

When Alexis had expressed all the concern and sympathy which he felt the subject demanded, he broached the question of Jenny's coming to school in Paris. Rose listened attentively.

"If you would like to know what I really think, Alexis, it seems to me that you have unconsciously invented the necessity of Jenny coming to Paris in order to get a good education. It is not necessary. The school at Chinon, just as in a hundred other provincial towns, provides as good, if not a better, education than any school you can find in Paris. And it has advantages lacking here. Jenny is precocious enough without growing up a little parisienne. As I say, it is not necessary. On the other hand, it is the only way in which you can see Jenny two or three times a week."

"Such an idea never entered my head," declared Alexis.

"I don't think it did for a moment. We conceal these plots from ourselves. So it all really boils down, in my opinion, to whether your happiness or her father's is most important. Naturally I should adore having Jenny here and she would fit in perfectly. But

George would be wretched if you uprooted him and I don't think I should be happy at leaving him alone. Jenny keeps an eye on him and sees he doesn't do silly things. She sees that he changes his clothes if he gets wet or overheated. When she is there he doesn't drink too much *marc*, as he would if he were alone. In fact, she is my deputy. So I think George is more important than you, and the plot you have been hatching unconsciously must be squashed."

Alexis was furious, but a long experience of negotiations with Russian staff officers had taught him to conceal his emotions. He remained unmoved, changed the subject and soon afterwards took his leave.

When he went down to *La Grange* as usual for the vintage in the following October, he found that the position had completely changed. Sir George had discussed the subject with Rose and had insisted that Jenny should only stay another term at Chinon. Then she was to go to Paris. Sir George would come also, at all events for the winter terms. He was seventy-seven and needed someone to keep an eye on him, as he said himself.

Alexis was delighted, but he refrained from saying so. At all events the matter had been discussed and settled and without his forcing the issue. Jenny was delighted too, but she did not conceal her feelings.

"I shall see you every day: you will introduce me to all the Generals and Admirals and perhaps, one day, you will employ me as your secretary."

The first evening after Alexis arrived he and

George were sitting on the terrace, looking across the valley to the Château de Couldray standing up in the rays of the setting sun. Rose was writing letters close by and Vincent was in the kitchen behind them cooking a dish of *piperade*. Jenny had disappeared upstairs.

George was a little stiff in his movements and slow in speech. But he held himself upright and still did light work in the vineyard. As the old man sat silently gazing across the valley with a glass of his wine untasted at his elbow, he seemed to Alexis to have scarcely changed at all while he himself had turned into a middle-aged man. The presence of Vincent, who had come back apparently cured from Switzerland, made him more aware of his age than he would have been otherwise.

"Good evening, Colonel. Will you be an angel and shake me up a dry martini?" drawled a childish, intentionally affected voice, speaking English, but rolling her r's.

Turning in his chair Alexis saw, coming towards him across the terrace, a figure wearing a white and silver lamé evening dress. He gazed for a moment puzzled: it had all happened before. With an effort Alexis shook himself out of his dream: yes, he had last seen that dress when Rose had put it on to impress his uncle when he had suddenly appeared at *Les Pervenches*.

It was extraordinary. Jenny might be Rose. And then he suddenly remembered his uncle's heart attack. The sight of the dress might kill him now. Somehow the child must be got away without attracting the old man's attention. Alexis held up his hand with the gesture of a policeman halting traffic. Then he put his finger to his lips. Jenny stopped dead, puzzled by his action and by the expression on his face. She had expected him to throw himself into her make-believe game of grand society. Next moment Rose saw her and put down her pen as she stood up with an expression of concern on her face. Sir George turned round.

"Jenny," said Rose in a penetrating whisper. "Go upstairs and take off those clothes at once."

Jenny hesitated, startled, and her father said with a delighted chuckle: "What a magnificent visitor we have here." He stood up and bowed deeply. "Will you allow me to take you down to supper, your ladyship? I am told that you are one of the new women and that you even think George Meredith *vieux jeu* in your set. I for my sins am completely *fin-de-siècle*."

Sir George chuckled a little at his own joke, which nobody else would see, while Jenny stood uncertainly and glanced at Rose.

"Oughtn't I have worn it, mother?" she asked.

"Well, perhaps this once," said Rose uncertainly.

"Surely you don't mind Jenny wearing one of your old stage dresses, darling? But which play was it? I can't for the life of me remember," said Sir George.

The question was left unanswered, for in response to an almost imperceptible nod from Rose the child held out her hand and drawled:

"You've saved me from a most embarrassing situation, Sir George. But I have no appetite for supper. Let us sit out this dance in the conservatory and I will toy with an oyster."

"May I have the pleasure of a dance," said Alexis, coming forward. Jenny took his hands and he gently fox-trotted her off the terrace. Directly they were out of ear-shot, the child looked him in the eyes and asked: "What's wrong? Tell me the truth."

"I will tell you later. But I think it would be better if you went up and took off that dress."

"But you must explain why."

Alexis nodded and followed her upstairs. While she was taking it off he said:

"You see, it belonged to Delia, your father's first wife. Once Rose put it on a great many years ago, before you were born, and the shock gave George a heart attack. So when your mother and I saw you wearing it we were afraid it might happen again. Luckily he seems to have forgotten it."

"Thank you for telling me," and Jenny, stepping out of the dress in nothing but her little pants, put her arms round Alexis's shoulders and kissed him on the lips.

"You are almost as tall as your mother already," he said, disengaging himself, and went downstairs.

"Why have we lost our great lady?" asked George as Jenny came and sat down at the supper table in her usual frock.

"It was too grand for the *piperade*," said Jenny.

"Well, I'm damned. You are an ungrateful brat," said Vincent, wounded in his *amour propre*.

After supper the child went and put her arms round Sir George and hugged him before kissing him goodnight. Her father ran his fingers through her tangled hair.

"You'll be the belle of the ball in another four or five years, my poppet. Goodnight. Sweet repose. All the bed and all the clothes." The last words were a formula which he repeated every night. His old nurse had used the incantation seventy years before. He had never asked himself why. "But next time you dress up in your mother's stage frocks, ask her first."

Jenny swept past Alexis with a wonderfully scornful air. "Goodnight, Colonel. Come up and see me sometime," and she gave Alexis a very meaning wink.

Half an hour later he acted on the invitation and found her sitting up in bed in pink pyjamas and her hair plaited in a pigtail.

"It was all right really about the dress, wasn't it?"

"Quite all right."

"I couldn't have known, could I? But Rose seemed very *piano* at supper, I thought."

"You notice everything."

"I can understand her being worried if it's what you said, but why did she go on being upset after he hadn't recognised it? Please explain that. It's so hateful living among a lot of mysteries and not knowing what one may do and what one mayn't."

"Well, Jenny. I think it was like this. First she was terrified lest he should have a heart attack. And then, when she saw he had forgotten all about it, she was upset because he had forgotten."

"You mean he forgot because he's so old?"

Alexis nodded.

"He forgets everything nowadays," said Jenny. "Yes, I think I understand. It's horrible."

"He would tell you that it wasn't horrible but natural and that you mustn't mind it," said Alexis.

Jenny nodded, her eyes bright with tears.

"I love you," she said, and held out her arms to be kissed.

"What do I find here?" said Rose as she came in to Jenny's bedroom. "Kissing and hugging and flirtation. Really, you are a shameless pair."

An hour later, when Alexis and Rose were talking quietly, Vincent was unobtrusively washing up with Gabrielle, and George was dozing with Vilmorin's catalogue in his hand, there was a cry from above.

"*Maman, Maman*, when are you coming up?"

Rose sighed, got up and went upstairs.

"What is it?" she asked in severe tones.

"*Maman*, will you promise to keep a secret? I'm in love with Alexis."

"Do you want me to tell him so?"

"Good God, no. He'll understand when he sees me fading away. Or I'll tell him myself. But don't you think he is the most adorable, kindest, handsomest man in the world?"

"I've seen more men than you have, darling."

"What a beastly thing to say. Oh, *Maman*, you are horrible."

Rose laughed, kissed her daughter and went downstairs.

"Bedtime, George. Remember, the vintage starts in earnest tomorrow."

"I've been dozing. Good gracious, it's ten o'clock."

The following evening they were all sitting on the terrace; Alexis and Rose and Jenny were so tired that they sat in luxurious passivity, for they had been picking grapes with only an hour's break since sunrise. George was tired too, though he had not worked in the vineyard but had occupied himself with the saccharometer testing samples of the must.

"Delia had a dress very like that one you put on last night, Jenny. I kept wondering all the afternoon about it. I wonder if by any chance it could be the same one," he said quietly.

Rose was amused and secretly delighted at her daughter's passion for Alexis and spoke of it to George.

"I've noticed it coming on for some time," he said. "And I don't like it at all. It's difficult to know what to do. I am very fond of Alexis, and coming here obviously means a lot to him. But Jenny comes first and we must stop this infatuation."

"I hope you won't try to interfere. You'll only make Jenny terribly unhappy."

"Alexis is such an unscrupulous character. I don't trust him. It is entirely his doing that we are being uprooted and going to Paris."

Rose stared in astonishment. It was George, not she, who had insisted on the Paris school. But she said nothing.

"I think when we settle there we shall have to tell him that we don't want him hanging around all the time."

"Why are you taking this line, George?"

"Well, I think these precocious emotions are bad for the child."

"Try and analyse your personal feelings."

Sir George said nothing.

"Isn't it just jealousy because you love Jenny better than anyone on earth and Alexis is a younger man?"

"No, I don't think so. I'm not jealous of Vincent."

This was undeniable but it was not a subject that Rose wished to discuss. If she had been driven to say what she felt, she would have said: "You are not jealous of Vincent because you are no longer in love with me. But you are in love with Jenny." And if pressed to define her relationship with Vincent she would have said:

"The whole thing is absurd and I really mean to put a stop to it. It means nothing to me." Sometimes, indeed, that was perfectly true, but at other times, when Vincent came into the room, she felt her heart beating with a delirious joy. And then she told herself that the reason was purely physical. But to go into all this with George would have been impossible, and so she laughed and said:

"Don't be silly," and added hastily: "You can't forbid Alexis to see Jenny without her finding out. You will make a charming piece of nonsense into a terrible tragedy and you will create all sorts of emotions not at all suitable for a child of thirteen."

Rose's last words were hypocritical. She knew well enough that practically the whole range of human emotion was inevitable at the age of thirteen and that nothing could be done about it.

Sir George took some time before replying. At last he said:

"Of course I was not suggesting *forbidding* Alexis to see Jenny. There are *nuances* in such things. But I will think over what you have said. You may be right. I certainly do put Jenny's welfare before that of anyone else in the world."

"I rather think Alexis does also."

"But if I may say so without being accused of ulterior motives, that is either a whim on his part or because he has feelings for a girl of thirteen which are bound to make us anxious."

"Don't be a pompous goose. It doesn't suit you."

Sir George was silent. At last he said: "I know I'm jealous and I know I'm old and going gaga. But

I'm not happy about this business of Alexis and Jenny."

Rose went up to him and, taking hold of his ears, kissed him rather brutally.

"You are the most unscrupulous old scoundrel. If you can't play one card, you quite shamelessly try to play another. But you are not to bitch everything when we are all as happy and as innocent as can be imagined."

"Oh, my darling. It is a relief to be able to speak perfectly freely. I expect you are quite right," said Sir George. "Now run along. Don't keep your young man in torture any longer."

Rose drew a deep breath, bared her teeth and almost spat at him.

"My God, if it weren't for that weak heart of yours I would tear you limb from limb. You sometimes go too far." Rose got up and, ruffling George's hair, went off to the room where Vincent was already fast asleep.

But although Sir George was persuaded to do nothing to interfere with Jenny's spending all her time with Alexis when he was at *La Grange* and writing to him two or three times a week when he was not, he was unable to hide the jealousy which had suddenly begun to devour him, and in a few weeks what Rose had foreseen had come to pass and the damage had been done.

Jenny loved her father more than her mother, but she had always been a little reserved with him. But for Alexis she felt passionate adoration. He was the only person to whom she told all her thoughts and feelings and in whom she had complete trust. Now she did not hesitate to speak to him of the unhappiness which her father's attitude was causing her.

"All fathers always behave like this to their daughters," said Alexis. "It is a law of nature which has to be accepted. Read Shakespeare and all the other poets. Actually your father is very fond of me, but he worships you and he cannot help feeling jealous. He knows quite well that it is comic and grotesque to have such feelings. So you must not resent them or be angry but try to help him overcome them by showing him how very much you love him."

"He makes it impossible for me to show love when I am feeling furious with him for sneering at you, or trying to interfere in my life," said Jenny.

"When has he tried to interfere? Do be fair."

"Well, he would like to, which is just as bad."

"Oh, no, it isn't. It is childish for you to be furious. You are growing up to be a woman, and women are always having to deal with unreasonable jealous men."

"You have never been jealous like that, have you?"

"Oh, my sweet Jenny. George is a saint compared with me," said Alexis. "I don't want to tell you about it now. It hurts me to think of it. But I will one day."

Jenny was silent, divining that another mystery lay behind her father's feelings for his nephew.

After Christmas, when the vines had been pruned

and the labourer was ploughing in manure between the rows, George and Jenny went to Paris, where Jenny would go to a new school. Rose had taken a little room high up under the roof for her. She and Vincent were to share the big bedroom and Sir George would occupy the spare room.

Alexis saw Jenny two or three times a week and Rose encouraged their friendship, but Sir George grumbled.

"Jenny is only thirteen. She ought to have friends of her own age. This passion for a man of forty is unhealthy."

Rose smiled at the exaggeration of Alexis's age. Sir George knew as well as she did that he was thirty-four.

"She's only been in Paris for a few weeks. It takes a little while to make friends at a strange school. Meanwhile, we ought to be grateful to Alexis for taking her about. Neither of us has the time or energy to do it. He is a perfect cavalier for her."

"Our room is always swarming with young people, but Jenny shows no signs of being interested in them," said her father.

It was true. But the young men and girls who came to the studio scarcely looked at the tall *farouche* child with disconcertingly steady grey eyes and sullen mouth.

Jenny was proud of being a child and avoided wearing clothes that looked grown-up or using lipstick or nail varnish like the "half-baked creatures" as she called them who swarmed round her mother. She spent much of her time in her room upstairs.

"I've some home-work to do," she would say. Really she wanted to be safe from the interruptions caused by actors, film stars and Rose's admirers. Sir George was often miserably unhappy, but he was old. He knew that there was no cure for age and he spent a surprisingly large part of the twenty-four hours asleep.

On Saturday afternoons it became the custom for Alexis to take Jenny to a picture show, or to a new play, or to a film. On Thursdays, a school holiday, he would often arrive after breakfast in his car and they would go off for the day into the country.

One night when they came back after seeing *Les Précieuses Ridicules* at the *Comédie Française* Jenny whispered to him in the courtyard in Rue Christine:

"Don't let's go into the studio. Come up to my room and kiss me, before you go."

Alexis nodded. As they went up, standing very close together in the lift, he felt his heart beating violently and he carefully avoided touching the lovely young creature beside him.

Once they were in her room and she had closed the door, Jenny put her arms on his shoulders and her soft young mouth to his. Then she seemed to collapse.

"Don't leave me, don't go away."

When at last Alexis gently disengaged himself, Jenny undressed, slipping with modesty into her nightgown. When she had got into bed, he stroked her hair, kissed her again and went away.

Alexis did not see much of Rose, but one day when he went to call for Jenny, her mother was alone.

"George has taken her out to lunch," she said. "They aren't back yet. By the way, I've been meaning to ask: what footing are you on with my daughter?"

Alexis hesitated and Rose continued: "I don't want to be unduly inquisitive, but it is better if I know what the situation is."

"I don't know if I'm in love with her. But I've never had such a pure feeling of devotion for anyone."

"You alarm me by that word *pure*. What exactly do you mean by it?"

Alexis looked at her angrily and turned pale, but when he spoke his voice was gentle and hesitant.

"I don't mean I have no physical feelings for her. One isn't supposed to feel them for children. I suppose it is abnormal. But I do feel them. Only they are completely swamped by my love and by knowing that I could never hurt her or do anything which could hurt her."

"Well, that is rather a relief," said Rose.

"I wasn't thinking of my physical feelings when I used the word pure. All I meant was that whereas when I was in love with you I was determined to dominate you, my love for Jenny is absolutely free of any such desire. I care only for her happiness and that she should seize every opportunity to develop all her gifts. I think she is going to be a writer, or a poet."

"You say you care only for her happiness—but I am not so sure," said Rose. "How will you behave in four years' time if she falls in love with a boy of twenty, or if you suddenly fall in love with a woman of your own age?"

Alexis shrugged his shoulders. "It's a difficult question. I suppose it would depend in each case partly on who it might be."

"It is just the difficult questions one must ask oneself. For example, how should I behave if it were Vincent?"

"How much are you in love with that young man?"

Rose laughed. "That's another subject and another difficult question. Forgive me for this cross-examination but I'm glad we have had this talk. George is often worried and I stick up for you. Naturally I must know what I am letting us all in for. But so long as you know what your feelings are, I think it will be all right. I think you ought to explain what your feelings are to Jenny and why you can't go any further than you do."

The conversation was interrupted and Alexis was relieved. The idea of speaking to Jenny of his physical feelings for her was extremely repugnant to him, and as soon as he could, he forgot Rose's advice.

The spring came and Alexis and Jenny went together to see the tulips at Bagatelle. Summer came and they went back there to see the roses. On Thursdays Alexis took Jenny for a picnic, usually far out of Paris. Before leaving the city, they stopped at their favourite *charcuterie* and Jenny would hesitate for some time before choosing from which *pâtés* she would buy a slice. In the *pâtisserie* she would spend an equally long time in choosing three little cakes or tarts. Then with a pot of *crème fraîche*, a bag of cherries, or alpine strawberries, a loaf of bread and a bottle of *muscadet*, they were sumptuously provided.

"Where do you suppose Alexis has taken Jenny?" Sir George asked grumpily.

"I expect they are at a film," replied Rose.

"What film?"

"How should I know?" said Rose.

But at that moment the shameless pair were lying side by side flat on their backs in the middle of a beech-wood thirty miles from Paris gazing at the layers of foliage, spreading like fans from the grey trunks. Only one or two spots of blue sky were visible through the canopy of leaves.

"Do you know that we are lying, not on our backs, but on our faces? We are lying on the deck of a boat and looking down through the seaweed at the bottom of the sea," said Jenny.

"So we are. It feels queer. Wouldn't it be awful if we fell in," replied Alexis.

"Look! There's a fish darting in and out of the seaweed, almost on the bottom."

"It's a very small fish."

"I like watching fish. They are much more interesting than birds," said Jenny.

"Fish-watching is much more fun than bird-watching."

Behind them, on the edge of the wood a nightingale began to sing.

"What's so nice about fish," said Jenny, "is their song. Birds are dull because they can't make a sound. But you can tell the fish apart, even when you can't see them."

Presently they got up and began to walk back to Alexis's little two-seater.

"I suppose we are at the bottom of the sea, now," said Alexis.

"Look out. Don't touch that hook hanging down there," exclaimed Jenny as Alexis was about to brush past a broken branch hanging across the path.

"The real danger is being trawled up. Look at that trawl flashing past. They are difficult to avoid," and Alexis pointed to a motor car passing along the road at the edge of the forest.

After Jenny's school broke up in the beginning of July, Rose and George, taking her with them, went to stay with Giulietta for a month and then spent another month touring about Italy. At the end of September Sir George went to *La Grange* to superintend the vintage and Alexis had to attend a military conference in the United States which occupied the whole of that month. Jenny had written to him regularly in letters full of descriptions of Venice and Rome and of wonderful Italian dishes, but they did not meet until his return to Paris in October.

Alexis was prepared for her childish passion for him to have become a thing of the past. At moments he told himself that it would be an immense relief and far better for them both if her feelings had changed.

However, when he rang the bell at the studio, Jenny opened the door and gave him one swift look. It was as though they had never been parted at all, and he suddenly felt deliriously happy.

Standing behind Jenny was Rose, who embraced him warmly. George welcomed him also and said how much he had missed him during the vintages, and asked him to stay to supper.

There was no opportunity for him to see or speak to Jenny alone that evening, but in the course of it Rose suggested that they should all go to the circus, and Jenny and Vincent took up the idea with joy. Though Rose had said: "Let's all go," she had assumed that George would prefer to be left behind. When the time came she was surprised to find that he was determined to be one of the party. The hour would be late for him and she guessed that he only wanted to come so as to be able to watch Alexis and Jenny, and if possible to prevent them sitting together.

"I think the recurrence of this obsession is becoming serious," Rose said to Vincent. "Will you arrange things so that when we take our seats, Alexis and Jenny go to the end of the row. Then you follow them; I will follow you and I will keep George beside me. Otherwise George's manoeuvres will drive Jenny crazy."

Vincent managed his commission with skill. But in the interval they rose to stretch their legs and to visit the cages where the performing tigers were kept and the ponies in their stables. Sir George, however, said he was tired and kept his seat. When they returned he arranged matters so that he was sitting on one side of Jenny and Rose on the other. But to Rose's surprise Jenny appeared unaware of her father's manoeuvre and laughed and talked excitedly to him between each of the turns. Many of them were beautiful and thrilling. Rose herself had a passion for trapezists and wire-walkers and sometimes declared that if she had to start life again she would choose to be an acrobat rather than an actress, as it should be possible to express oneself more completely with one's whole body than with voice and gesture.

At this performance there were layers of wire-walkers and trapezists extending very high up into the roof and they moved and flew about like so many rose-coloured angels busily carrying messages in the halls of Heaven. There were tigers and sea-lions and, most wonderful of all, half a dozen performing cats which at a given signal climbed up little rope ladders and jumped into baskets which came slowly down on pulleys.

When the circus was over they all walked together to where Rose had parked her car.

"Well, thank you all immensely. I'll take a bus home," said Alexis. Rose looked at Jenny and saw that her eyes were fixed on Alexis and that there was a peculiar little smile on her face. She made no protest as her mother had feared she might. "The little creature has some secret up her sleeve," she thought, but it was a blessing anyway that Alexis had had the tact to take himself off. Rose still thought of Jenny as *la petite*, though the child was half an inch taller than she was herself.

An hour and a half later Alexis went into the hall and rang the bell for the lift. He had entered it, and had just pressed the starting-button when the door of the studio opened and Sir George looked out. Alexis had just time to observe a look of consternation on his uncle's face when the lift started. He saw Sir George run out and then begin coming up the staircase as fast as he could. Then the edge of the *entresol* floor cut off his view.

It was obvious that if he went on up to Jenny's room and kissed her goodnight as he had promised, her father would come knocking on her door and there would be the kind of scene which, for Jenny's sake, must be avoided at all costs.

There were four floors and, following the rule never to act until he knew what he intended to do, which he had formulated in jungle fighting, Alexis did nothing for half a minute. Then he pressed the emergency stop button. He waited for thirty seconds to allow his uncle to climb up at least as high as the second floor. Then he pressed the ground-floor button. Sir George would see him going down in the lift and would go no further, and eventually come down again without seeing Jenny. Meanwhile he would have left the house himself.

But there was no sign of Sir George on the staircase or on the landings until just after the lift had left the *entresol* when he saw a body lying on the stairs. Alexis stopped the lift, went back to the *entresol*, got out and then ran down to where his uncle was lying. It was at once obvious to Alexis that Sir George was dead. But though he knew this perfectly well, he refused to admit the fact at once. He picked up the body, putting one hand under George's arm and another in his crotch and with a skill born of handling wounded men and helped by the fall in the stair, swung him on to his shoulder and then carried him downstairs to the ground floor. The door of the studio was ajar as Sir George must have left it and the lights were on in the studio.

"Rose, Rose," he called.

"What is it?" A note of horror sounded in her voice.

"George has had an attack," he said and, still balancing the body on his shoulder, opened the door of his uncle's bedroom. It was in darkness and he could not find the switch.

Next moment the door of the large bedroom was

thrown open and Vincent stood in it, naked under a mackintosh. Alexis turned to him and caught over the young man's shoulder a glimpse of Rose's naked limbs as she scrambled out of bed.

"Bring him in here," she said, and Alexis went in and, with Vincent's help, laid George down.

"Get one of his amine capsules," said Alexis. "But I don't think there's much hope."

Rose stood perfectly calm, grave and beautiful with a strand of her long hair hanging over one eye. Though completely occupied in finding out whether there was a spark of life left, Alexis noticed a grey hair in Rose's tawny fleece. He had never seen one there before. She had picked up the quilt from the bed and wound it tightly round her body under the arms like a Malay sarong, so that her powerful shoulders were bare.

She watched with a grave face while Alexis broke the capsule under Sir George's nostrils.

"There's no pulse at all. I don't think he is breathing. Give me your mirror."

Rose picked up a hand mirror and watched silently while Alexis held it in front of the half-open mouth.

"I suppose there's just a chance that artificial respiration would bring him round." With Vincent's help he turned the body over and began the movements.

"I can do that," said Vincent, and Alexis resigned the task to him.

"How did it happen?" asked Rose.

"I promised Jenny to come and kiss her goodnight

when we were looking at the tigers. George must have suspected something and have sat up to watch after you had gone to bed. Just as I started going up in the lift he came out of the door and began running up the stairs after me. I was afraid of a scene in front of Jenny, so I stopped the lift, waited a little and started coming down. When I got to the *entresol* I saw his body lying on the stairs."

"I understand. So Jenny knows nothing about it?"

"You had better ring up the doctor at once," said Alexis.

"I had better put on my clothes before he comes," said Vincent.

"Yes, we had better both be found dressed," remarked Rose. "But before I ring him we had better decide what to say and stick to one story. I think it is simple enough to say he had a heart attack when he was sitting by the fire, and we carried him in here." She rang up the doctor; then, with complete disregard of Alexis's presence, she threw off the quilt and began putting on her clothes. It did not occur to either of the men to leave the bedroom. While she was putting up her hair and powdering her face, Jenny opened the bedroom door and walked in. She was wearing her dressing gown.

"Your father has had a terribly bad heart attack," said Rose.

"How did it happen?"

"It just happened suddenly as he was sitting by the fire."

Soon after the doctor had come and announced that Sir George was dead, which all of them knew already, Alexis kissed Rose and Jenny and went away. He could not face getting into the lift and going up to Jenny's room a second time that evening. His first premonitions of evil had been fulfilled and he was still an irrational creature.

But next day when he and Jenny were lunching together at *Le Vert Galant*—he had thought food was the best consolation he could offer—she put down her fork and said:

"Why didn't Rose tell me the truth last night?"

"Didn't she?"

"How did you come to be there?"

"It happened just as I was going up to your room."

"What I don't understand is why the lift came nearly all the way up to my room. Then it stopped and waited and then it went down again. Then someone got out and left the lift door open on the *entresol* floor. I was listening, expecting you to come. It was you who were in the lift, of course."

Alexis nodded. "I'll explain, but not now. It's very simple, there's no mystery."

"But Rose was making a mystery. She was just finishing dressing when I came in and she had been to bed."

"Don't bother about all that. I've promised to tell you exactly what happened and I will some time. Now have a sip of your champagne."

That evening, after Jenny had gone to bed, Alexis

sat downstairs in the studio talking to Rose and Vincent. After a time he said: "Do you realise that I was entirely responsible for George's death?"

Rose shrugged her shoulders. "Why go into all that?"

"Because what am I to say to Jenny? You see, if I had stopped the lift when I saw him beginning to climb the stairs . . ."

"A scene with you was more likely to be fatal than anything," put in Vincent.

"That's perfectly true. The less said the better. Words don't help," said Rose.

"Jenny asked me about it today. I'll go up and say goodnight to her," said Alexis.

When he tapped at the door Jenny opened it at once. She was wearing a completely transparent nylon nightgown and her fleece of hair hung down to the small of her back. Her eyes were big, her face unusually pale.

"So you've come."

"Yes, I've come to say goodnight."

"Rose is the danger now. She wants us to give up seeing each other."

"Oh, what did she say?"

"She hasn't said anything. But I can feel it. She has changed. But nothing in the world will stop me seeing you."

She put her arms round his chest, hugged him and began to sob. Alexis held her tight so that she could not see his face. He had turned very pale and for a moment was scarcely master of himself. What was he to do with a child with the emotions of a woman? A child whom he loved as though she were a woman?

Presently Jenny relaxed her hold and sat on the bed gasping.

"I think I am going to be ill. I'll drink some water."

She tried to get up to fetch it.

"Get into bed."

Alexis pulled down the blankets and sheet, picked up the childish body, wrapped in its transparency, put her into bed and covered her up. Then he filled a glass of water, felt in his coat pocket and found a bottle of sleeping tablets.

"Take this."

Jenny swallowed the pill. "You won't go away, will you? Come into bed with me."

Alexis took off his shoes and jacket and got into the bed. There was very little room for them both.

"I want you. I want to belong to you entirely."

"Be quiet, darling."

"It's not as though I didn't know all about love, living in this house."

"Don't talk any more."

Jenny lay clinging to him so tightly that even after the drug acted and she had gone to sleep, it took a quarter of an hour before he could make her relax her grip so that he could slip quietly out of bed.

As he walked back to his hotel Alexis had such a bad headache that he had to stand still in the street two or three times, waiting for the wave of pain to pass off.

"What am I to do? What am I to do? It's serious," he kept repeating to himself.

When he got back to his room he found that there were three sleeping tablets left in the bottle. He took them and fell fast asleep. He did not go to the Rue Christine for the next two days. The day after that would be the funeral.

Part Five

Sir George had amused himself by planning his own funeral in great detail and Rose carried out his wishes exactly. His body was cremated at Père Lachaise without any of his friends being present.

His ashes were to be scattered in the vineyard at Seuilly which was to be the occasion for a party with wine, music and dancing. A great many invitations were sent out and a whole fleet of cars drove down from Paris. Alexis had been kept for an important staff meeting and drove down alone. It was already late afternoon when he arrived and the by-road leading to *La Grange* was black with people. He turned his little car into a field and joined the throng of peasants and neighbours walking up to the house. When he reached it, he was embraced by Rose, whose breath already smelt of grape kernels. She had been drinking *marc*.

The house and the terrace were thronged with actors, actresses, film stars, writers and artists. To his astonishment Alexis found himself being condoled with by the British Ambassador. As he parted from His Excellency, he noticed a small, lean dark-skinned woman with very beautiful eyes. He remembered that Rose had once said: "Cleopatra was a thin wiry creature." As he was looking at her she came up to him and said: "So you are the famous Alexis, whom I have never met. I am the Marchesa Trapani."

Alexis cast his mind back over the years and said: "Then you are Giulietta."

"Yes, I heard a great deal about you when Rose and George came to Venice, before their marriage."

"You mean when her arm was paralysed after I had shot her? I suppose you will be terribly disillusioned and disappointed if I tell you that it was really unintentional. But probably you don't believe me."

"No. Quite the reverse. I much prefer to think you were undecided and would have drawn the line at actually murdering her."

"*Trincquet*," exclaimed Vincent, handing them glasses.

A voice speaking English suddenly fell on his ear.

"Do I understand there are going to be speeches? It is really too bad of dear Rose to forget to warn me—I haven't prepared anything." It was a voice beloved by millions. Alexis turned and saw that the features were also beloved by millions on TV. He felt sick but he had often had the feeling listening to Army Commanders and he said nothing.

Alexis caught Giulietta's eye. She gave him a warm look, so intimate that not a word needed to be said, and then a little laugh in which there was a trace of embarrassment.

"Perhaps George should have chosen him instead of me," she said.

At last, half an hour before sunset, Rose and Jenny led the way from the terrace to the vineyard. The vintage had taken place three weeks before and the red-gold autumnal leaves, lit up by the setting sun, hanging thickly on the vines, made a blaze of colour. A thick throng of people encircled the vineyard. In the middle was a tumbril with a ladder, towards which all slowly made their way.

Suddenly Alexis saw that Giulietta had climbed up the ladder into the cart. Silence fell, and it was a surprise to him to hear her speaking in English.

"George Dillingham was unlike most of the men of to-day. He did not want to change human life, or human nature, or think it wise to attempt to do so. He rejoiced in the way we are made. He did not look forward to Heaven. He was happy with the earth.

"George combined the virtues of a man of antiquity with those of a man of fifty years ago. He had, like a man of the Renaissance, an insatiable appetite for life and a belief in its goodness. He loved and understood the flesh and believed that flesh and spirit are inseparable. He liked man to be an animal and had the vigorous instincts of an animal himself. He understood and loved food and wine. More than either, he loved and understood women and many women were enriched by his love. But unlike the men of the Renaissance, he was also a creature of great delicacy of taste and feeling. However passionate he might be, however strong his appetite, he was never selfish. He was always ready to think another might be right and that he might be wrong. He respected the individuality of others and he was the least arrogant of men. In the generation in which he was born they would have said that he had the delicate perceptions of a woman. If that was true then, it is no longer, for we women today have lost the delicacy of our grandmothers.

"Luckily both his gusto and his delicacy showed themselves in his work. He was not like any of the poets of today. He was nearest to the Latin poets: to Catullus and Petronius and to that poet, perhaps Virgil, who wrote the poem about the Syrian Dancing Girl, the last lines of which I shall read you because it was thinking of that poem that led him to plan this gathering of his friends. I shall read it in Helen Waddell's translation, for the majority of you here are without Latin.

Heigh ho; but it's good to lie here under the vines,
And bind on your heavy head a garland of roses,

And reap the scarlet lips of a pretty girl.
—You be damned, you there with your Puritan
    eyebrows!
What thanks will cold ashes give for the sweetness
    of garlands?
Or is it your mind to hang a rose-wreath on your
    tombstone?
Set down the wine and the dice, and perish the
    thought of tomorrow!
Here's Death twitching my ear. 'Live,' says he,
    'for I'm coming.' "

When Giulietta had finished speaking, there was silence, perhaps because the majority of those listening had not understood her words. Alexis felt uncomfortable because she had spoken in English, which seemed to him a fault in taste. After she had climbed down, there was a pause and then Marcel, who had grown enormously fat, began, with some difficulty, to climb the ladder. When he had done so, he bowed to the company and said: "My duty here is to repeat in French what our Italian friend, herself a noble lover of poetry and of poets, has said."

Without more ado Marcel delivered a translation of Giulietta's speech which he must have committed to heart. When he had finished he added a few sentences of his own. His words were delivered with perfect simplicity; he seemed to be speaking extempore and every word was audible to the most distant of the crowd. When he finished there was a murmur of approbation. There was some laughter also, as he was helped down the ladder.

Rose, carrying a box containing George's ashes and holding a large pewter ladle which struck a comic note, walked down the centre of the vineyard and began to throw spoonfuls of ashes among the vines. She was bareheaded with her hair hanging loose on her shoulders and was dressed in black.

When all the ashes were strewn, Rose turned to the company and said:

"Dear friends and neighbours of the Chinonais. If what I have been doing seems strange to you, I must remind you that I am carrying out the wishes of my husband. He made me promise to strew his ashes among the vines he loved. He asked that when that had been done everyone should drink his wine, that there should be music and then dancing and that the evening should end with the kind of happy party which he loved so much. Now we will listen to some music and I hope after that everyone will stay to dance and to drink."

Among the guests were several musicians who had come from Paris with their instruments. There was a flute player who also at intervals played the piccolo, another played the violin, a third the viola, a fourth the oboe and a fifth the bassoon. This group of four men and a woman began first with stately music, with Lulli and Loeillet. Then they passed to Mozart. By degrees the music grew gayer and gayer. Giulietta and Alexis were among the first of the dancers. The enormously fat Marcel was partnered by the *sage-femme* who had attended Jenny's birth, Vincent by the *La Grange bonne*, Gabrielle. Twilight faded into night, the terrace was flooded with light, but the dancers often passed into the darkness of the drive and the courtyard. On the edge of the lighted area were two barrels of clear, strong Chinon wine which had been three years in the barrels. Those who pressed round them drank from little pewter pans before they went back to the dance.

Alexis had stood beside Jenny when the ashes were being strewn but was separated from her during the music. After his dance with Giulietta he missed her and going into the house found her at the open window of her room.

"No, it's too much. I can't dance."

"You can. George was right. You can have two emotions at the same time. One makes the other even more acute and then cures it."

Alexis took her hands and led her downstairs and began dancing with her. By this time the Parisian instrumentalists, one of whom was world famous, had been joined by local musical talent in the shape of an accordion and a cornet from the village and two negroes, a drummer and a saxophone player, from the U.S. Army Engineering Depot on the far side of Chinon.

As in all truly successful parties one or two unknown figures suddenly appeared and attracted all eyes owing to their vitality and self-abandonment. One of these, a girl named Raymonde, turned out to be a cousin of Rose's and the daughter of a gaoler at Fontévrault, one an American boy called Gordon who sat beside a wine barrel drinking, and when apparently quite drunk, walked into the centre of the terrace between two of the dances and began to recite Rabelais' delightful verses designed to be written up on the main doorway of the Abbey of Theleme, from chapter fifty-four of *Gargantua*. It was obvious that Gordon had a good knowledge of fifteenth-century French. He put a wealth of hatred and contempt into the early verses which catalogue those who will not be allowed to enter.

> *Cy n'entrez pas, hypocrites, bigotz,*
> *Vieux matagotz, marmiteux, bersouflés,*

but when after exhausting the list of scribes, pharisees and *Grippeminaulx* lawyers, he came to the list of those who would be welcome, his voice changed, the signs of drunkenness disappeared and he spoke in tones almost of ecstasy:

> *Cy entrez, vous, dames de haut paraige!*
> *En franc couraige entrez y en bon heur,*
> *Fleurs de beaulté, à celeste visaige,*
> *A droit corsaige, à maintien prude et saige.*

When the dancing began again, Raymonde took hold of Gordon and they began dancing with such fury that most of the other couples stopped to watch and to applaud. When the dance was over they disappeared and were seen no more till supper.

After two hours the dancing stopped. Long tables of boards supported on empty barrels were put up and trays of food put on them. Everyone helped himself to whatever came nearest. The lucky ones got piping hot *bouchés* filled with minced chicken, *fonds d'artichaut*, mushrooms and cream. While they were eating and talking, many people became aware that the autumn air was chilly and were glad to begin dancing again as soon as the music struck up. Older persons were delighted to find a roaring fire had been lighted indoors, and ate roast chestnuts.

"Come, let's get away. I can't stand any more," said Jenny. Alexis took her arm and they walked away into the night as far as the big mulberry tree where they sat down. Three minutes later Jenny was fast asleep. Alexis went back to the house and returned with a pillow which he put under her head and three rugs which he tucked in round her without waking her.

Not far away he could hear murmurs and movements among the vines. As he went back to the party, he met two couples coming away from it. They walked into the vineyard where the black silhouettes of heads and shoulders moved above the rows of vines. When he looked again after a moment they had disappeared.

As Alexis stepped into the circle of light he found Giulietta beside him.

"Shall we dance?" he asked.

"No, I've danced enough," she replied and suddenly he saw the lovely black almond eyes fixed upon him and his heart beat fast and he felt himself turn pale.

"Come for a walk," he said, and she nodded.

"How can this be happening to me so simply?" he wondered. A moment later they were shadows in the darkness. He led the way across a meadow and she followed in silence until he reached the cow-byre where he paused at the bottom of the ladder leading to the hay-loft.

"Let's climb up here," said Alexis.

Giulietta gave a quiet laugh of pleasure, almost the gurgling note of a nightingale. Hearing this Alexis put his arm on her shoulder and the next moment she was in his arms. The embrace lasted for a long while. Then he climbed up the ladder and pushed open the heavy trap-door. Giulietta followed him and he lowered it.

"Stay with me."

"I must go now. I left Jenny asleep under the

mulberry. I don't think she ought to stay there all night."

"You stay with me, now."

"I will go and see if she is all right, get her into bed and then come back."

"When you come back you will stay with me, to-morrow and tomorrow and tomorrow. For ever."

"Do you mean it?"

"I shall take you back to Italy with me. You must be ready to come with me."

"Will you stay here till I come back?"

"Yes. But do not be too long putting that child to bed."

Alexis lifted the trap-door and lowered it after him as he went down the ladder. There was the sweet scent of a cow's breath and he could hear the two animals munching in the darkness. He hurried back towards the farm.

"Have you seen Rose?" Vincent asked him as he went into the circle of light.

"I saw her at supper. Not since."

After looking everywhere, Vincent went upstairs and found Rose lying alone on her bed with her face buried in a pillow.

"Are you feeling ill, darling?"

"Go away, Vincent. I want to be alone."

"Are you sure you are all right?"

"Go away. I don't want you. I mean it."

Vincent went away. Five minutes later Marcel, who

had eaten and drunk and danced more than he had meant to do and was feeling a little sick, came into her room looking for somewhere to rest.

"Why, it's Rose. My dear, you mustn't cry like this."

"Why not? I can't help it."

The immensely fat man, baulked of his desire to lie down himself, drew a chair up to the bed and held Rose's hand while she went on weeping uncontrollably.

Later on, as people kept coming into the room, apologising and going out again, he got up and locked the door.

"That poor fellow Vincent suspects me and is ready to think I am Rose's lover. Thank God, I am spared that complication at all events," Alexis said to himself as he walked quickly to the mulberry tree. Jenny had thrown off the blankets and was stirring.

"I thought you had gone away and that I was alone," she said.

"Come, darling Jenny. It's late and you'll catch cold here on the bare ground. You must go to bed."

Alexis helped her up and supported her, for she was still more than half asleep. Then, carrying the blankets and the pillow, he led her back to the house and took her up to her room.

"Who's there?" asked a girl's voice in the darkness.

"It's Jenny," said Alexis. He switched on the light. It was Rose's cousin Raymonde and, slightly to his surprise, he saw that she was alone.

"Gabrielle said that you would not mind me sharing your bed. She could not find anywhere else for me," she said. "I hope you don't mind."

Jenny stood blinking in the light and made an effort to wake up.

"No, of course not. I am sorry to have disturbed you. I'll be in bed in a minute."

"I shall be gone before you wake up," said Alexis.

"Oh, you didn't tell me. I hoped you would drive me back," said Jenny, disappointed.

"I have to be in Paris by lunch-time. Much better get a good sleep. Goodnight, darling."

Jenny was shy in front of Raymonde and did not kiss him. As he hurried away he could hear someone weeping in Rose's room. "I hope that little brute Vincent isn't making a nasty scene. But it's not like Rose to be reduced to tears," he thought. He walked slowly back to the cow-byre. There was nobody about.

Giulietta was asleep and he slipped down beside her in the dry lucerne hay. The effects of the wine he had drunk had long since worn off, or perhaps the claims that Sir George made for his vintages were justified. His head was clear and he lay awake feeling torn in two. At all costs he must prevent Jenny from finding out what he had done, but was it possible? It might have a horrible effect on her. Yet every fibre tingled with the triumph of having won Giulietta. If, when she woke up, she still wanted him to go to Italy with her, if she wanted him tomorrow and tomorrow and tomorrow—he could not possibly give her up.

If she meant her words literally, what would he say? Would he sacrifice his career in the Army? Yes. Yes, with joy. That meant nothing, had meant less and less in the last few years. But Jenny? Putting aside all thoughts of Giulietta, he must face the future of his relationship with Jenny. At fourteen it was still possible to treat her as a child. But it would become harder with every month and year that passed.

Even if he could resist her at fifteen, could he trust himself when she was sixteen, or sixteen and a half and her physical passion for him increased?

To seduce her would be criminal. Was it less criminal to break her heart? It was frightening that he already felt bound to deceive her, if he had a relationship with another woman. And the nearer they came to being lovers, the more necessary such deceptions would become. Where was he heading? Was George's death to be only the first of a series of tragedies? No. He would go away.

Whatever Giulietta might feel for him, he had made up his mind about Jenny. From that moment he felt at peace with himself. He wondered why, an hour before, he had felt torn in two. Everything was simple. It was dawn. Giulietta had turned towards him in her sleep: her long black hair hanging loose about her face was full of little bits of dry lucerne leaf. It would take ages to brush out. Her face was calm, the twisted aquiline nose rather predatory, the mouth with a full lower lip rather too small, the fine forehead noble and intelligent. There was scarcely a wrinkle on her face, yet he could see she was a woman of about forty: a few years older than himself. Their love-making had left him feeling very tender and protective towards her, but at that moment he could not tell if he had fallen in love with her or not. Meanwhile the sooner that he was on the road the better. He did not like to wake her, yet he could not steal away without giving her an opportunity to come with him. If she did not come, he must know where to find her again.

At last he bent over and kissed her on the cheek. She turned to him, opened her eyes and drew him to her.

"Darling, we really must go now. Do you still want to come with me?"

"Of course."

They stole out. The cows rose and rattled their chains and looked at them expectantly. There was a thick mist filling the valley of the Vienne and all the lower ground. A woman's shoes and a man's waistcoat were lying on the terrace where they had been discarded. They helped themselves to some broken rolls of bread on the table and each drank a panikin of wine from one of the barrels. Alexis half-filled an empty bottle from the barrel and then they walked down the lane to the field where he had left his car.

It was a long way from the house and nobody could see them driving off.

When Alexis rang the bell of the studio about midday on the following day, Jenny opened it and let him in. She said nothing and did not kiss him. Rose and Vincent were sitting at the breakfast table in dressing-gowns. Marcel was there too.

"I came to take Jenny out to lunch and find you still having breakfast," said Alexis.

Rose looked at him and said nothing. There was a change in her.

"Have a glass of *porto*?" said Vincent. "We are just getting to that stage."

"I'll be ready in five minutes," said Jenny and left the room.

"What have you done to Jenny to upset her?" asked Rose.

"Nothing so far as I know. She fell asleep under the mulberry. Later I took her indoors and up to her room where she spent the night with Raymonde."

Vincent pulled a cork and filled glasses.

"*Trincquet*," he said. Alexis did not take the glass.

"Well, I'm worried about you and Jenny and that's a fact," said Rose.

"I don't want to discuss it. I shall deal with the situation in my own way," said Alexis.

"You make it impossible," said Marcel.

Rose suddenly gave a tremendous yawn so that Alexis could see all her teeth. She was forty and had never needed to go to a dentist except to get her teeth polished when they were stained. She was like a tigress yawning in the zoo.

"A man-eater," thought Alexis. "Who called her that and when?"

"Well, Marcel wants me to go and rehearse in a bloody awful play. I must put some clothes on." She got up and went into her bedroom and shut the door.

"Rose is really rather worried," said Vincent confidentially.

"Everybody's worried except you," said Alexis.

Startled by this asperity, Vincent gave a faint giggle, and Marcel looked at him with surprise.

"I don't believe in worry. *Trincquet*," said Vincent.

Jenny opened the door, dressed ready to go out.

Alexis nodded to each of the men, got up and walked out of the room with her, shutting the door behind him.

"Let's go up to your room. Don't use the lift. It makes a noise and I want to talk to you seriously without their knowing," said Alexis.

When they reached her room Alexis saw that Jenny was looking frightened. It was with some difficulty that he repressed the desire to kiss her and forced himself to speak.

"Sit down, Jenny. I want to talk seriously. The last time I was in this room you said that you were in love with me and that you knew all about love and wanted me to be your lover. But that is quite impossible. You have the body of a child, not yet ripe for love. Tormenting desire, ecstasy, all the communion and relief of physical love are yet to come. And they can only come naturally, when your body is not only formed, but ripe. You may think I am being cruel, but I am only being truthful. Nothing is worth saying but the truth which we must face."

"Go on."

"Not only is your body not ready for physical love, but your heart isn't either. It would be wicked to force you into unnatural feelings."

"They aren't unnatural. I shall never believe that. What about Juliet? What about Bettina and Goethe and . . . and . . . and . . . you know . . . it wouldn't be unnatural."

"Darling, I didn't mean your feelings were not strong and genuine. Only that they are different in kind. You aren't a woman and love is a thing that mustn't be forced."

"You've said that already. It isn't forced. It's here."

"Please be patient with me. I don't mean to deny your love. But I must use that word unnatural again. Our love, mine more than yours, is unnatural because it cannot, or at any rate, it must not express itself. And intense passionate love must express itself physically, or else the body takes revenges on the soul and we become monsters."

"Is that why . . . you and Giulietta . . . when I was asleep?"

Alexis sat petrified and said nothing. After a long pause Jenny went on: "Gabrielle told me she saw you both come out of the hayloft when she was going to go milking. And then I went there and saw the mark where you had been making love together in the hay."

Alexis said nothing.

"And then you both went away together before anybody was awake, except Gabrielle. And ... and ... and ... are you in love with her?"

"I am not sure. But I should be saying just the same to you now, if I had never met her."

"Well, say it. Say I am a child and ... and I can't make love like her and ... and ... and ... I can't even feel it. Go on, say it. That's what you came to say, isn't it?"

"It's part of it, I suppose," said Alexis.

"And ... and ... do you know what I should say? I should say that when people grow up they all seem to be at the mercy of their bodies ... and I am not sorry to be only a child if that's what being grown-up means."

"The difficulty is that you are no longer a child and that you are not yet a woman. You are fourteen."

"Older than Juliet."

"Yes. But you must not have a lover for four or five years. In that time anything may happen and your feelings will change. Meanwhile we must part."

"Do stop talking. I want to think."

This remark completely unnerved Alexis. His

words, determined on before-hand, had carried him along. The last thing he wanted to do was to think and now, completely at sea and lost, he remained silent. Nor had he the faintest idea what was passing inside that tawny head, bent with the eyes fixed on the floor.

"What were you going to say?" she asked at last.

"That we must part, for my sake, just as much as for yours. I dare say that your feelings aren't unnatural. But mine are in danger of becoming so. It is unnatural for a man to feel desire for a child and it must be repressed. If I acted on such feelings I should quite properly be put in prison."

At these words Jenny made a movement of incredulity and exasperation which to his annoyance reminded him of Rose. She was the last person he wanted to think of.

"And yet when . . . when . . . when you loved my mother . . . you were ready to face going to prison . . . when you shot her."

"Oh, my dear. How long have you known that?"

"I overheard Marcel and *Maman* talking together soon after I came to Paris. And then I asked her. She wouldn't tell me until I threatened to ask you and then she said it was her fault more than yours and made me promise never, never to speak of it. And . . . and . . . now I've broken my promise . . . Does it matter very much?"

"No. It doesn't matter at all. Only I wish I had known that you knew." They sat silent for a long time. At last Jenny said: "You don't think I don't love you because you loved Rose, and because you thought it was better to die together than to live apart? I loved you just the same even when I saw that mark in the hay ..." She could not go on speaking and began to sob.

Alexis waited for Jenny to get some control of herself. At last he said: "Will you promise, since you love me, to put me in the back of your mind while you go to school and later when you go to college? I am leaving Paris and don't know when I shall come back. But I am sure to come here and we can go to a theatre and have lunch sometimes. And you can always write to me and no one will see your letters ... and I will write to you." Alexis had not intended to say a word of this but could not help himself.

"I suppose you are going to marry Giulietta, I would rather it was her than someone I didn't like. But if you don't, will you marry me, or let me live with you, if I wait four years?" This was a question that Alexis had anticipated and was dreading. He knew that he must not say yes. And it would be needlessly cruel, perhaps even dangerous, to say no. He held out his arms and Jenny flung herself upon him.

When, almost an hour later, he walked down the accursed stairs, he remembered the phrase that his uncle had used to him at Pau.

"Ce sera un souvenir léger pour toi."

"Well, anyway I had the grace not to say that to her. Perhaps long before four years are over it will be *un souvenir léger* for Jenny. I suppose that I hope it will. But not for me."

He walked down to the *quai* where his little car was parked with Giulietta in it, reading *Concluding* by Henry Green.

She shut the book and smiled at him.

"I'm famished. It's a quarter to two. Let's have lunch and I won't ask any questions."

"I think I have broken Jenny's heart but you have saved me from committing a horrible action," he said when they were having dinner together that evening at St. Dizier.

Giulietta opened her dark eyes very wide and looked at him.

"There is something very extraordinary in our situation," she said. "And that is that we should be in love. Because we provide each other with the only solution to an impossible situation."

"What do you mean? I can see what you provide me with. But I don't provide anything . . ."

Giulietta interrupted him.

"While George lived I could never be in love with any man for more than a few months. I was like Sir Thomas Wyatt's girls:

> *but now they range
> busily seeking with continual change.'*

But I shall be faithful to you."

"But were you in love with my uncle?"

"Of course I was. You know my husband, Orlando, was killed in a car accident on our honeymoon? George was the first man I met who understood about that and talked to me about him. I loved him for his kindness. But Rose never gave me much of a chance. She dominated him, as I suppose she dominated you."

"No. She taught me, what I always thought George taught her: that the worst kind of misfortune is to be Blake's pebble:

> *'Love seeketh only self to please*
> *To bind another to its delight,*
> *Joy's in another's loss of ease*
> *And builds a hell in heaven's despite.' "*

"But I always thought your love for Jenny was a sublimation of your desire for revenge on George and of your passion for Rose."

"You are entirely and absolutely wrong. I love Jenny for her own sake and my love for her has never had anything to do with either of them. When she was a child we were perfectly intimate and I could be happy without wanting physical love in my life. Now she is growing up and during the change from child to woman the relationship has become impossible."

"So you are giving me warning that I must look out for squalls in five years' time."

"I hope Jenny will be in love with someone of her own age, then."

"I suppose you think you do hope it. And yet I am quite sure you don't," said Giulietta. Alexis said nothing and presently Giulietta held out her empty glass and said: "*Pone merum et talos. Pereat qui crastina curat.*" Then, as Alexis had obviously not understood her, she repeated the Latin sentences in English:

> "*Set down the wine and the dice*
> *and perish the thought of tomorrow.*"

THE END

A NOTE ON THE TYPE

This book was set in Fournier, a type face named for Pierre Simon Fournier, a celebrated type designer in eighteenth-century France. Fournier's type is considered transitional in that it drew its inspiration from the old style yet was ingeniously innovational, providing for an elegant yet legible appearance. For some time after his death in 1768, Fournier was remembered primarily as the author of a famous manual of typography and as a pioneer of the point system. However, in 1925, his reputation was enhanced when The Monotype Corporation of London revived Fournier's roman and italic.

Composed by Crane Typesetting Service, Inc.,
Barnstable, Massachusetts
Printed and bound by The Haddon Craftsmen,
Scranton, Pennsylvania
Designed by Virginia Tan